NATURAL FREQUENCY

A Book of Short Stories about Life & Magic

Derek Finn

FNP

Frogsnotpigeons

ISBN-13: 9798639344749
ISBN-10: 1477123456

Cover design by: Nicola Chestnutt
Library of Congress Control Number: 2018675309
Printed in the United States of America

For those who live for magic in their lives

All men have the stars. For some who are travellers, the stars are guides. For others they are just lights in the sky. But for you, you alone have the stars as no one else has them.

CONTENTS

PREFACE

Some people, for many reasons, can find it difficult to express themselves. Here is a group of short stories told through a particular lens that uses humor and sarcasm to convey a positive message to the reader. Each story tells of a particular aspect of life but is told as interpretive so that the reader may take meaning applicable to themselves or their life circumstance.

The main characters are the Witch, the Pigeon and the Frog. Each represent certain traits that carry through the stories. For example, the Pigeon represents hope and the Frog represents sadness and regret. Read as the Witch holds on to the 'Pigeon' and pushes the 'Frog' aside.

I hope that you enjoy the stories for what they are intended. That is, as a group of short stories with light hearted meaning.

We are frogsnotpigeons. Join Us.

THE ACCUSATION

The local villagers have gathered to demand a meeting with the Witch. Lots of rumours that the Witch is involved in the disappearance of the skinny local bookstore keeper and wannabe blogger, Arat, now missing for at least three days. The Witch and her simple brother McNnif are both in attendance at the village meeting with about twenty of the locals. The town folk are mostly settled Vikings, who gave up the pillaging lifestyle for farming some years back. Stocky looking bunch with unkept hair and hairy faces. And the men are just as rough.

"Witch, we want answers as to your involvement with the disappeared woman" cries a burly brute in the front row that opens proceedings. The Witch is sipping on her flat white not in any rush to answer questions from this mob. The question is repeated. This time slightly louder and with a sense of growing urgency. The hall is lit by the light of many candles and the flickering glow makes the audience look, well, menacing. "What proof do you have of involvement by my sister in the disappearance of the skinny woman"? shouts the Wizard McNnif.

"It is known that the Witch cast a spell the night of her disappearance" calls out a Viking from the crowd. "There is but one Witch in this village and no one else that could magic the disappearance of the skinny bookstore keeper". The Witch has put her coffee cup down to stand slowly from her chair. "Who is accusing me?" she asks her eyes flashing in the flickering light. A large Viking steps forward, his food stained shirt riding up over a proud hairy naval, with a loud and beery voice that booms a stunted response… "I do Witch".

The Witch walks slowly and deliberately to the centre of the hall ringed by onlookers on all sides to face her accuser. Candlelight dances up the walls and there is a haze of burnt wax hanging in the air. The blond hair of the Witch, like gold straw contrasting against her black sweatshirt and a pair of high heels left over from a previous occasion, looks up at her accuser. "Ah – Ronald Double-Cheese, the man who can eat a bale of hay. I tell you all that the skinny woman is not disappeared. I saw her reflection in my glass ball only some two days ago". A loud mumble goes around the long hall as the Vikings consider the rebuttal. "None the less Witch, do you deny that you put a spell on the skinny one at the same time of her disappearance?"

"Look it, I thought she was having an affair with my man, and I asked for a friend to pay her a visit to find out the truth" explains the Witch. "I have since found out that she was not seeing my man. She is probably reading one of her books in a cave somewhere if not eaten by Ronald here in front of me for lunch".

Being different does not mean that there is something wrong with you. Sometimes, people want to be busy finding faults with your life instead of fixing their own. Be who you are first and let others pretend to be someone they are not.

Suspicious Minds

Some time later, the Witch has retreated back to her own home and sits at the Kitchen Table musing on the events of the week with her companions.

"I can't put up with your suspicions anymore, constantly questioning for meaning in meaningless events. I don't want to be part of the soap opera running in your head" Robert tells the Witch. She doesn't look up from the table and is instead focused on the Pigeon sitting on the table. "I may be broken", she mumbles, "but I provide all that you need. You cut, and I am bleeding, but I loved you with my whole heart".

"Why do you speak in this useless metaphor language"? asks Robert his head bobbing from side to side, so annoyingly! The Witch doesn't respond, with her back to Robert, she wipes a tear from her eye. A silent moment between the two, just another shared in the growing distance between the pair. The Pigeon is the first to break the silence and starts to flap wildly.

The Witch holds the bird, gently, just enough to prevent flight. "You think more of that flipping bird" shouts Robert his voice raised through frustration.

"This Witch act is becoming tiring; you have fabricated a persona to suit your crony friends who cackle at the sight of a full moon" he continues sarcastically. Coming closer to the Witch, he reaches to place his hand on her shoulder from behind. As though by radar, the Witch senses the movement and releases the Pigeon airborne while simultaneously standing and turning to Robert. He hesitates at the sudden movement and is now standing face to face with the teary-eyed Witch. The Pigeon circulates the pair like a hysterical hyena with wings.

Robert is motionless feeling his eyeballs widen at the unfolding events and the challenge of the Witch. With that, as though swatting at an annoying fly, Robert makes a failed swat at the Pigeon circulating overhead causing feathers to launch. His attention drawn to the bird, he prepares to launch a new intervention to stop the birds flight.

The Witch has repositioned herself, ensuring at least an arm's length from the agitated Robert. "Chords and Sensor, Scourge and Knife, by all the power of the Witches' blade, as I do will so shall it be, cast this spell and be it done" echoes out from the sullen

Witch.

A sudden flash of light and then, well, nothing....

The room is silent, the bird has landed on the Witches shoulder and Robert is no more to be seen. There is a light haze of what looks like incense smoke lingering in the space and an unusual scent that smells like damp leaves. The Witch raises one hand and strokes the plume of the Pigeon as though stroking the fur of a cat. Coo... Coo... the Pigeon sounds in contentment with the action of it's master.

On the floor, at the feet of the Witch, a pool of water and little webbed footprints leading away towards the back door.

You choose who is in your life. But remember that those who constantly want to find fault with your life, also want you to be as unhappy as they are.

◆ ◆ ◆

The Cloak of Night

The Witch is not happy. Stroking the pigeon, she alternates between heartbroken, because Robert is gone, and relieved that the affair is over. She'd finally rid herself of that nagging man. She is also bone-tired of the Villagers who seek to blame her for various disappearances. The same Villagers who incessantly beg her for spells, fortune reading, potions and other Witch stuff.

Outside, the wind blows as the first of the Autumn storms arrive. The night turns blacker. The fire throws flickers of light dancing throughout the small room. The pigeon coo'd restlessly under her rough stroke. Then, she hears a sound.

A whistle. Faint. Lilting. Almost on the edge of being.
The pigeon stilled as they both hold their breath. Waiting for the

sound to repeat.

There it was! A little clearer, yet still distant. The Witch forgets about nursing her grievances and puts her attention to the hearing of the delicate sound. As her thoughts quiet, the whistle grows softly louder. Its lilting music conjuring visions of green meadows and running streams. She gives herself to the hearing willingly finding a comfort in the sound. A green cloak, dark as the deepest forest shadow, appears draped on the chair next to her. She carefully sets her favourite teacup on the table and reaches out to touch the warmth of its heavy, soft wool, heedless of the fact that no such cloak was there a moment ago. She notices a blackthorn staff resting next to the cloak and a small lantern glowing softly nearby. Time and thoughts cease. In an instant she stands, wraps the cloak about her, and takes up the staff. She reaches for the lantern just as the pigeon moves to nestle itself into the pocket of the cloak. Lifting the lantern, she noticed that instead of a ray of light, the lantern throws stars about the room, illuminating the area with an ethereal glow. A path appears. She steps forward.

The next morning, the Simple Wizard McNnif decides to check on his sister. He thought he might catch her in time to coax her into cooking breakfast. He knocks. Usually his sister is up at this hour nursing her second cup of tea that made the Witch a little more approachable. He knocks again, louder. Becoming worried when a third knock elicits nothing but a deeper silence. He tries the handle. The door is locked. Reaching into the flower pot for the spare key, he cautiously opens the door.

Nothing but emptiness greets his entrance. The cottage looks as if abandoned for years. The sight of a thick coat of dust, a startling amount of spider webs, a musty odour, and the Witch's favourite teacup overturned on the table is all that answers his call out. This is unusual. And disturbing.

There was nothing for it but for the Wizard to get himself to the

Pub and announce his unnerving discovery to anyone who would buy a pint and listen. By midday everyone knew. Everyone wondered. Everyone worried. They only miss you once you're gone.

'The Fountain of Frogs'.

Over the last week, the town is inundated with a plague of frogs that has taken over the fountain at the centre of the town piazza. The timing of this amphibian invasion could not be worse with autumnal wind raising dances of leaves across the square. With incessant croaking, the little green creatures appear to be taunting the leaves into more and more elaborate displays with the wind.

After repeated attempts from the town residents, no one has dissuaded the creatures from taking up new residence in the piazza fountain. If anything, the number of creatures appears to be increasing as each night passes with nearby residents forced to close windows at night-time for fear of unwelcome amphibian house guests. However, despite repeated warnings to residents not to approach the frog hoard, there is always one, one who will not heed warnings. A Viking woman, Togram, has decided she can no longer accept the disturbance to her Monday night TV viewing and will resolve the 'frog' issue herself. As you might imagine, several residents think this could be more exciting than the current series of 'Somewhere has got Talent', and prefer to watch the live show unfolding, Viking versus Frogs, play out. The Viking, armed with a witch's broom, sweeps in across the piazza in what appears to be an attempt to catch the frogs by surprise. Her first move gathers a large swathe of frogs up in the broom and they are thrown back to one side. The frogs respond in a unison of croaking that is almost deafening followed by leaping and jumping over one another to claim back the paving stone made clear by the broom.

To the cheering delight of the on-lookers, the Viking has adopted a defensive stance waving the old witch's broom above her head as though preparing a mass strike against the green creatures. The sight and sound of the spectacle is so mesmerising to participants and spectators that they have just noticed the sudden appearance of two cloaked and hooded individuals now standing in the centre of the sea of angry frogs. As one hooded stranger raises an open hand to the night, the broom held aloft by the Viking woman leaves her grip and appears to float through the sky to the open hand of the cloaked individual. The frogs incessant croaking has stilled to silence. The Viking woman is enraged with the uninvited interference of the pair of strangers in costume. "This is not your business" calls the Viking "be gone now. Come back next week for Halloween".

The pair of hooded strangers join hands and a low sound of chanting grows louder as the two recite simultaneously. The Viking steps back as she feels the swath of frogs surrounding her feet melt away, like bath water retreating, back towards the pair of strangers.

In minutes, the piazza floor that was once covered in green, is cleared back to the paved stone floors. The Viking and the spectators feel the eerie silence of night again and although wondering, know for sure that the Witches are home.

Real friends are never far away when you need them.

THE WITCH'S FOLLY

Halloween Night. Our Witch is at the annual get together of the coven. It's a closed affair with only Witches and the odd drop in present. Something like a ladies night out for the local womens group without the handbags and makeup. As the circle is made, east to west and north to south, each of the Witches holding hands to close the circle, looking skywards, each fall to a trance. The only sound is the crackle of the fire burning in the grate and the unison sound of heartbeats beating as one. Thum Thum... Thum Thum... Thum Thum.... Thum Thum..

Let the nights journey commence.

Our Witch sees now only from her mind's eye as she lights up the Halloween sky. The now familiar whistle sound beckoning her deeper into the night. The lantern lights the way in her mind like a tunnel to a place reached only by a few. Her thoughts become still, and time has stopped. The only connection to the outside, a small movement occasionally from the Pigeon nestled in her cloak pocket. Silence envelops our mind travelling duo.

Eventually, the pair arrive at an open space with a large tree surrounded by sweet grass. Her vision is filled with the sight of the tree limbs outstretched from one end of the horizon to the other. The lanterns light is soft now, fading, as the Witch rests from her journey among the ferns and the grass. Tired to her bones, she wraps the cloak tighter to her body, with Pigeon close to her breast for comfort.

A rustling sound behind her startles and she turns quickly. A large Stag with antlers raised high stands square. Breathing mist from its black nose. Holding the staff tightly in one hand she recognizes the Stag as the Horned Hunter and duly bows her head to the magnificent creature. Even the Pigeon is held to silence at the sight of the magnificent creature before them.

"What is your intention here this night"? booms the Stag. The Witch lifts her gaze from the ground to look directly to the Stag. "We are here to ask of you Horned Hunter" she responds in a soft but confident tone.

"Speak now Witch" booms the stag.

"I have spent so much time with my only companion this Pigeon, tell me where will I find happiness that I can lift this veil of sadness that I have worn for too long now"? Instinctively, dropping her gaze to the ground.

The Stag acknowledges her benediction and shakes his powerful shoulders from side to side. The Witch drops the staff from her grasp to place both her hands firmly on the soft ground as though seeking balance or to feel the surety of the ground beneath her. Motionless, she feels a deep rousing inside her. Her shoulders soften, relaxed and her breathing shallow. The Witch feels a deep peacefulness envelop her.

After minutes that feels like hours, the Witch opens her eyes and finds that the Stag is no longer present and instead a tall man with hooded cape to cover his face.

"The happiness you seek is already within you" he speaks.

The Witch's Reflection.

With Samháin over, there is a sense of preparing for winter. At home with her broom, the Witch and the Pigeon are tidying autumnal leaves from the garden under fading light when a reflection in the garden pond catches her attention.

The Witch crouching low, peers into the water and into her own eyes caught in a sort of mindfulness trance. As she continues to stare, she notices the movement of clouds across her own reflection like clouds across the face of the moon. She moves closer to the reflection; with an index finger extended she reaches her hand towards and into the watery image. Circle paths ripple across the surface of the quiet water ever expanding. Close your eyes now and you will see them.

Then, like a bird to flight, she takes to the sky. The sounds around her magnified by the thin night air that envelopes her. As she becomes the darkness, faces of many glance momentarily by, calling out but not heard, as though car headlights heading in the opposite direction on a busy motorway. She lets out a triumphal scream with joy as she passes beneath the clouds not feeling cold, not feeling anything except the wind rushing past her cheeks. The moment continues for some minutes until she hears a voice calling her through the wind. Ever so faint, a voice calling her Irish name softly from a distance. The Witch slows her sky travel and starts to focus effort on hearing this voice.

As the sound becomes clearer, the Witch is transitioned back from the wind and night sky to the garden pond where she finds only the Pigeon present.

"Who is calling?" cries out the Witch to no answer. Only the Pigeon breaks the silence with a Coo... Coo... noise as they do. From over the Witch's shoulder, and from a dark corner of the garden steps forward a young woman dressed head to foot in the Cape of Mórda. As the Witch jumps to her feet, she suddenly feels a sharp drop in temperature and her breath is turned to fog in a dim light. "What is your business here?" calls the Witch expectantly, sensing the power of this woman.

The Cloaked woman steps out of darkness towards the Witch. With each step, the garden grass is glistened over with a layer of frost danced on by a harvest-moon glow. The Witch and the Pigeon back away slowly. The cloaked woman makes a sweeping gesture with her hand to the air and a vision appears over her shoulder of a high mountain ridge. "Come to the edge" calls the cloaked woman. "Come to the edge, bring your Pigeon" she calls again.

The Witch has recognized the voice. "We are good this side" calls the Witch back. "You have been missed down at the book-store you know".

If your searching for that one person that can change your life, take a look in the mirror. It starts with you first.

◆ ◆ ◆

The Last Taxi.

The Witch and her brother Simple Wizard McNnif are in the village today to pay their respects on the passing of one of the village elders and part time taxi driver.

Always a solemn occasion these last goodbyes and this is no different. The Viking clan are in attendance, but they also go to the opening of an envelope if there was a free drink and food involved.

As the Witch and her brother enter the funeral hall, the brother leans to his sister "perhaps you should remove the tall pointy hat". As she does, her strawberry blonde hair unfurls across her shoulders in contrast to the blackness of her cape like a wave breaking on a distant beach. Can you see it?

Since the deceased was also the village part time taxi driver, the hall is filled with all sorts. But mostly drinkers, present to show final respects and wondering how to get home afterwards. Thirty minutes later and the ceremony is concluded. The rabble file out of the hall to the large bonfire lighting outside at the back of the hall.

The fire mostly constructed of wooden pallets, is crackling and sparking like some angry nymph creature throwing fire and smoke high into the night sky. I love a good fire, thinks our Witch to herself, it's like looking into one of those snow globes, except its hotter.

The Vikings have circled the fire and are dancing to a single drummer drumming out a rhythmic beat in a regular 4/4 beat.

The mourners file past the immediate family with the usual platitudes from strangers, awkwardly looking for something comforting to say. "It was sudden, he was only ill for last 6 years" or "he's gone to the happy place now" or my favourite, "he looks so well dead".

The Witch and her brother Wizard McNnif are charged with leading the group chant as the final passing ritual. As the time approaches the mourning group are circling the ebbing fire looking skywards as she commences the chant. As she concludes there is a large roar from the gathered Vikings, their own way of saying goodbye.

As the Viking hoard dissipates back inside to the promised re-freshments, the Witch stands alone, mesmerized by the dying fire, reflecting on recent events and the meaning in her life. Her brother decides to give her space and follows the Vikings back inside.

The night sky darkens as the Witch now stands alone. Her tall hat pointing to some distant star above. As she drops her hands to her side, she notices that there is someone standing beside her. A man, strong, tall, physical, cloaked in the gown of a high priest. His scent is on her breath and she breaths it willingly. He catches the Witch by her hand, and she feels the warmth and comfort in his grip. "Don't let go of my hand ever again" he speaks. The witch reciprocates by a small squeeze of his hand.

Life is a choice. It's your life. Choose wisely and honestly. Choose happiness.

◆ ◆ ◆

The Witch's Heart.

'She is acting very strange lately, going around smiling at stran-gers. No one likes a loved-up Witch especially coming up to black Friday.' Speaks Togram the Viking Woman, muttering under her breath. Like most Viking women, Togram has an opinion of others and likes to have her own way. Her best feature is prob-ably her long hair that would do proud any racehorse. The Simple Wizard McNnif in contrast, is a quiet soul with a receding hairline that exposes his forehead making him look more intelligent than he really is.

As the pair arrive at the cottage, they find the Witch sitting in her chair humming along to some tune playing from her phone with the Pigeon perched on her shoulder like a scene from some pirate movie. Togram makes here presence known and the Witch turns to acknowledge the visitors with her eyes and a broad smile.

'Welcome Viking, I sensed your presence near before you arrived' calls the Witch. 'Do take off your cow skin wrap and join me by the fire'. Accepting the invite, Togram de-robes of the cow skin. 'The simple Wizard thought he heard music and singing as we arrived?' exclaims the Viking. The Witch just smiles back intentionally without responding.

Togram takes an armchair beside the Witch facing towards the fire. There is radiating heat from the fire hearth that is felt on the face of the two women who stare almost expectantly into the dancing fire light. Do you feel the heat on your face?

The Witch reaches her hand across to take the hand of Togram in a rare moment of connection shared between two strong women. 'I know why you are here' says the Witch. Togram turns towards the Witch quickly, but just enough to catch a reflection of the fire blinking in her eyes and a broad smile across her face. Suddenly, the Witch rolls her eyes back and squeezes the rough hand of the Viking Woman. The scene is instantly changed to bright sun light and broad expanse of white sand beach. Togram looks to the blue sky wondering how she has been transported to this place but feeling the warmth of the sun on her face, is content and at peace with her unexpected surroundings. Just above the shore line is a large standing stone depicting a snake with an inscription along its body. Togram recognizes the script language instantly as from her own tribe. "Your visions become clear only when you look into your own heart".

As quickly as they had arrived, the scene turns to night and the sky is alighted with the crystal sparkle of starlight. As Togram stands beside the Witch she can feel her strong heart beating in the stillness of this star night. A deep calmness fills both women. The Witch turns her gaze from the sky to the Viking Woman and in an instant, both are transported back to the living room and a man's voice breaking the silence.

'Did you want milk with your tea?' asks McNnif.

Some people will cross your path and change your life direction.

BLACK FRIDAY

Many Vikings have invaded the local village for the black Friday sales. The village and its shops are crowded with Vikings looking for bargains as though stocking up for endless winter.

However, it's not just the Viking Hoard, the Witch and her frogs-notpigeons crew is also in town looking for bargains.

'What do you think of this? calls the Witch back to the witching crew, at the same time holding up a large cauldron pot above her shoulder. A resounding cackle of approval from the frogsnotpigeons is enough for our Witch to decide its needed to go with the other 27 pots at home. As she makes her way to the queue for the checkout, she notices that there is some pushing ahead in the queue.

The dispute quickly spreads, and others get involved. Our Witch decides to step back from this brawl. As she does, her black hat is knocked to the floor, and in the ensuing melee, trampled under-foot by the hoofed feet of the Viking hoard. The pushing and shoving escalate to an all-out scrum with skin, fur and feathers flying in all directions. Just then, a small group of men dressed in grey cloaks held with a large metal broch and wearing tight fitting trousers appear at the doorway. If you can visualize a boyband on their second comeback tour that would be close.

However, the Witch recognizes them only as Northern Viking guards. With a banging of swords to shields the noise is enough to get the attention of the disputing women fighting over a hair dryer on sale. 'Silence!' shouts the bigger of the guards and the ensuing brawl is quenched as faces turn towards the guards standing in the doorway. 'Everyone must leave this place and disperse' is the next instruction. Almost as quickly as the dispute started, there is a disgruntled but orderly evacuation of the store. As everyone assembles outside the store, the Witch realizes that her black hat is still inside on the floor. She must have this back and approaches the nearest grey cloaked guard. 'My hat is on the floor inside' she speaks. Abruptly the guard turns to see who has the nerve to address him while performing his duties. 'My hat is on the floor inside' repeats the Witch in a soft but assertive tone. The guard almost dismisses the young Witch but instead has caught the glisten of her steely blue eyes with his. 'Who are you woman? 'he shouts through his bearded face in a strong tone with a northern accent. Our Witch is not so accustomed to open challenge but steps closer as she feels the strength of her hooded crew arrive at her side. 'We will not dance tonight Viking' she whispers softly to the guard's ear.

Sometimes in life, we just need a hug. No words, no advice. A quiet hug makes you feel you matter.

Goddess Danu

The time has come to appoint a new village elder. As is tradition, the elder will be of the Tuatha De Danand Tribe – also known as the People of the Goddess Danu. Our Witch is pleased with this decision as these are her folk and she will travel to attend the ceremony.

For company, the Witch brings her Pigeon and the Frog Robert with her on the short travel to pay her respects. On arrival, the Witch is formally welcomed into the ceremony hall and takes her seat in the round chamber. There is a full house of fifty Witches at this ceremony each seated around the outer wall of the chamber to form a large circle. They all sit in silence as a mark of respect to the presence of the Goddess Danu. But if you listen closely now you will hear them breathing...

At the centre of the room, the seated Druid is approached by the Danu Priestess and struck firmly with a wand of ash. This immediately gives the Druid the power of prophesy, a vital skill for a village elder. A tall young woman in silver gown approach's the centre of the room carrying in front of her a large bowl of rose petals. As the Danu Priestess recites her spell, she places her hand on the shoulder the young woman who is instantly changed to a scarlet fly. This fly is the size of an apple and the sound of its buzzing and the beating of its wings create a hypnotic effect in the chamber so all who can, hear. The Priestess continues her spell 'as long as this fly is with you, you shall not take another wife. The fly will always stay by the side of the elder, it's colour and fragrance to satisfy any hunger and quench any thirst. A drop of water from its wings to cure affliction and disease. And with your life, you will protect the fly from harm for if you should lose the fly, you will become a pool of water and be deposed'.

Like a good wedding ceremony, except in this case the bride is a fly and the groom an old druid, the Witch is watching the ceremony with tears in her eyes. 'I love a good ceremony' she speaks out loud to herself wiping a tear from her eye. 'We should congratulate the old druid on his appointment' she muses to the Pigeon and Frog.

'Congratulations' she whispers and bows her head in reverence. 'Nice looking bird' he smirks referring to the Pigeon on her shoulder. 'Thank you so much' she blushes and instantly takes the frog out of her cloak pocket 'and here is his companion Robert' she says proudly. As the Druid peers into the Witches outstretched hand, the frog rolls its eyeballs, and as though taking a deep breath, launches its tongue to wrap around the fly and with a large gulp, it is gone. In an instant, where once stood the proud druid is now a pool of water.

Sometimes life doesn't follow the plan. How you respond to life events is your choice.

◆ ◆ ◆

Match Making

'OMG – another visitor to the door' she cries out. 'What is it with people nowadays who want to visit on a Sunday?' Over the last two weeks there is a significant increase in visitors to the Witch looking for various interventions such as card reading, potions, spells and an assortment of dietary advice.

'Are you home Witch'? cries the next visitor from the front door-way left open by the last visitor. Into the kitchen walks a burly woman with large clogs on her feet and wild unkept hair. She has the shoulders of a ploughing horse and teeth to match. 'Yes, I'm home. What can I do to help you on this lovely Sunday and day of rest for everyone else? starts the Witch in a slightly sarcastic tone.

'Well, I wanted to speak to you about a spell to use that will help me to become a fair maiden again so that I might find a suiter to bring me to the local dance'. The Witch has heard this request a couple of times so is not overly surprised to hear these 'Cin-derella' requests as she calls them. However, this one is slightly different in so much as the challenge will be greater. 'Tell me more horse lady' inquires the Witch. 'Well, I have three sisters all who spend their time talking about their make-up, what they will be wearing and how they will do their hair. I feel at times that I am left out of this conversation as I don't have someone to bring to the dance' she continues.

'And what else?' probes the Witch.

'Well, my sisters spend a lot of their time on frogsnap constantly posting pictures of themselves – and then making fun of how I look that really upsets me. I have a part time job in Makky Dee's in the town that I don't really have time for the frogsnap group.' With that the Pigeon makes a flapping noise as though to exercise his wings after a snooze or perhaps a sympathy vote.

A large crash on the door disturbs the session and the Viking Chieftain Oran has burst in through the Kitchen door. His flaxen like hair, wild as though a constant storm rages in his head and his white cloak make him a formidable character. 'How dare you interrupt my sessions here at my home' roars the Witch back at the large Viking man. The Witch's demur is so small compared to this brut but nonetheless she has squared up to the big man. 'I swear by all that my people swear by, that you shall not take access to my place at your will' she screams into his face with her eyes wide as though about to explode from her face and attack.

However, the Viking Chieftain has fallen silent and is instead staring towards the woman seated in the corner of the Kitchen. As though the storm in his head has finally passed, his head tilts slightly and a toothless smile is forced across his weather-beaten face.

No one decides who is beautiful and who is not. Wait for the right person that releases the beauty in you.

Moon Dancers

The nights have turned so cold recently and tonight is no different. There is a full moon that is casting its silver light down on to the forest below so that the trees look like silver and the leaves frozen decorations from a Christmas tree.

In a small clearing towards the centre of the forest there is a small gathering of like-minded individuals in their cloaks and tall hats.

Around the outer perimeter of the clearing are the flying banners, like warning signs, displaying the blue pigeon with a red eye, the symbol of the goddess 'Epona' whose name means 'Moon Dance'.

At the centre of this circle is a standing stone with old Celtic symbols of the Tua De Dannan. The assembly have formed a circle around the stone holding hands in a chain link form and chanting in unison words of a foreign tongue. The circle is rotating left one step every couple of bars of the chant that looks like a subdued version of line dancing.

The stepping action and the breathing of the assembly creates a rising of fog that lifts above the tree line like a mist of silver glistening by the moon light.

The chanting sound is mesmerizing, forming a rhythmic pattern repeating over and over like the heartbeat of a large animal. Thum Thum... Thum Thum.. Thum Thum... listen now and you will hear it.

Throughout the surrounding woods there is silence. The usual habitants holding their own peace as the foreign visitors hold their conference of night. No creature will disturb them intentionally.

Our Witch breaks the circle and steps to the centre of the ring. Arms held to the sky she becomes the night and takes to the sky like a bird to flight. All the circling witches of frogsnotpigeons, cry out in unison as though cheering their colleague skywards. Every living thing in the forest knows this sound. A local huntsman from the village is walking towards the forest humming some Christmas song and hears the Witches cry. He knows the sound and not to approach the gathering. Looking skyward to the moon he sees the silhouetted image of a bird, or to be exact, the Pigeon with a red eye.

Stars can't shine without darkness first.

HEART TO HEART.

Taking to flight at night is emotionally draining for any Witch. During these trips, there is no thoughts, no concept of time. Focus is on breathing and the mind is still like a high mountain lake and its mirror surface. In this state, the Witch is one with the sky and nothing else. Something like a mindfulness session outdoors while balancing on a thin broom.

The Witch is home with the Pigeon and the Frog relaxing before the holiday sets in proper. This is always a time for family and friends and still, for some, a time of finding their place with others.

With her shawl wrapped tight across her shoulders, 'tell me Pigeon, what are you thinking about - I sense your restlessness'.

With blue feathers touching her skin, the Pigeon coo's. 'I am thinking, am I here by my choice or because you brought me to this place?'

The Witch blinks as she stares back at the Pigeon's single red eye. 'Maybe bird we are destined to be where we are in this place, together. I hope maybe you'll come where I am going'.

The Pigeon looks back confused. 'I just need an open door so that I can breathe again. I need to stretch my wings and fly towards the sun on the horizon when I want to'.

'Bird, the innocence in your face, has left you. You are no longer a squab and instead a full-grown Pigeon. Your eyes are not drier than mine. Your soul survives looking for a peace that I still hope we can find together'. With that, the Witch jumps to her feet and opens the back door. The bird is blinking on the table looking to the early morning sky and an openness that means a new life. Hesitancy hangs in the air as though a fog descending in the kitchen. 'You have a choice bird but know that I don't want you to go' she says fighting back tears in the doorway.

I can't imagine what things would be like if I hadn't met you. Sniff.

Remember, you don't need to be alone to be lonely.

◆ ◆ ◆

Quick Hands

A youth from the village is waiting to see the Witch on a matter of urgency. The Witch beckons him inside. The house smells of burnt candle wax but is warm with the remnants of a wilting Christmas tree still standing in the corner. She nods her approval for the boy to speak.

'The Spirit Queen visited me last night in a dream' he starts. 'I saw myself in the forest with a red deer at my feet. The Spirit is telling me to tell you that I am a great hunter and I want to leave my school.' After a minute the Witch asks. 'How can you be so sure of this dream meaning? After all you are not a tarot card reader and did not attend the lesson when the opportunity was offered'. The youth thought for a second. 'Because I am destined for bigger things than any school can teach' he responds with surety.

The Witch lets the silence exist between them and casually throws some herbs onto the fire. 'It is well known that Dream Weavers do not speak straight – maybe the dream meaning is something else' she speaks.

'No!' the youth interrupts. 'You are not listening woman to what I have said. The Spirit has sent me a message to give to you that I am to be a hunter and you are to make it so or ignore the Spirit at your own peril'.

The Witch looks the youth in the eye 'maybe you are right, for you are much younger than me, quick witted, strong of heart and quick thinking'. The boy nods in agreement and stands expecting the Witch's agreement. 'Come to the fire when the moon is at her highest and show me your skills' she says.

At high moon, the youth makes his way to the Witch's Circle gathered at the fire. Stepping from the shadows the boy announces his arrival confidently and steps into the circle of cloaks known as the frogsnotpigeons.

Listen, as the Witch speaks: 'This young man was visited by the Spirit to tell him that he is a great man and we are foolish to ignore this message sent by the Spirit.' The youth turns full circle and then back to face the Witch. 'I am ready, to accept the appointment shown to me in the dream'.

The Witch reaches an antler into the hot embers and with a flick of her wrist fires a red-hot ember towards the youth who instinctively reaches and catches the hot stone in his hands. In pain, he drops the stone and turns in anger towards the Witch now standing. 'You stupid Witch, what have you done, I have burned my precious hands. The Spirit will visit regret on you tonight'.

A wise person knows when to dodge danger. A good sport knows how to react to a poorly played game. A good person with a strong heart knows humility.

Perhaps the dream sent by the Spirit represents something else after all.

Frog Sense

The frog had a confused look on its green face. The Witch, who had visited the pond every morning for many moon phases seems different today. Her shoulders were slumped, her feet dragged, and her smile was the wrong way around.

Since the frog was a tadpole, the Witch visited the edge of the water every sunrise. There, she'd greet the sun with her arms raised, feel mother earth beneath her feet and give thanks to the water spirits. The frog had grown to appreciate the daily visitor and enjoyed watching this water side ritual. The Witch's happiness and appreciation became the frog's happiness and appreciation.

However, over the last few days, the Witch appeared at the water side distracted with her arms folded, staring down at mother earth, dragging her feet, ignoring the sunrise, ignoring the frog. The frog was understanding of the Witch's worldly responsibilities and wished the Witch would be happier after the next sunrise.

The next morning, the sun rose high in anticipation of the new day, and as frog had done many other times, waited patiently for the Witch to appear. Recognising the same sadness on her face the Frog decided to dive to the bottom of the pond to have a think himself. After a while, the frog surfaced with his bulging eyes above the water to see the Witch still at the water's edge.

'Where did you go? I was worried!' called the Witch to frog. The frog, who was surprised by the Witch's concern, calls back: 'Sometimes we all need to quest for answers. If I get stuck with worries on my mind, I like to swim to the bottom of the pond and bury myself in the mud.... it helps me connect to mother earth. It helps to comfort me through difficult times. But not too long under water otherwise I drown!' With that, the frog hops on to the mud bank and stretched out in the new sunlight. 'Sometimes I also do this – sitting in the sun sending my gratitude for all I have and feel the sun connecting back to me through the comfort of the sun's warmth. But not too long otherwise I could dry out!'.

The Witch shakes her head; 'So what's the point frog, you can't stay under water and you can't stay above water long either, what are you trying to tell me?'

'When your caught by worry or fear, its best to move. Find quietness if you need to, but only on your terms. Use it to find the answers you need but don't stay in the quiet too long for its easy to become trapped if we wallow for too long'.

The Witch smiled in understanding and offered the palm of her hand to the frog. Thank you frog for your wisdom she said gently as she lowered to let the frog jump to a lily pad.

PIGEON POWER

Moonlight is flooding the forest floor, casting shadows to the ground from tree branches that dance with the breeze of the night forest. The Witch and the Pigeon are visiting their favourite listening tree near the heart of the forest. As the pair make their way along the darkening path, they happen upon a fallen tree across the path and a faint cry of a distressed animal.

As the pair get closer, the Witch notices deep brown eyes staring back from under the leaves and branches of the downed tree. Shaking with fear, it is the face of a young deer trapped by the branches of the fallen tree. The Witch moves her hands to clear the face of the deer, brushing away the leaves from its face. The deer blinks its large brown eyes and exhales a shallow breath that sounds as though there will not be many more this night.

The Witch places a hand on the deer close to where its heart is. She feels life ebbing from the frightened creature. The Witch feels an emotion that she has not felt for many years. So many thoughts run through her mind; How all of life is precious and that every living creature is connected – no one soul is more or less than the other. Wiping a stray tear from her face, the Witch stands to see that a heavy branch of the tree is across the animal's delicate body. Blinking back her own tears, the Witch turns back to the animal, leaning close enough to let her tears fall to its face and eventually, to Mother Earth herself. 'Tell me what to do,' she whispers, 'you are too precious to end here'.

The Witch hears a response, but does not recognize the voice as her heart floods with emotions that have been kept hidden for so long. 'Opening your heart that is closed for so long is the bravest of things....choose to feel again and you can do so much'. At first the Witch thinks that the deer has spoken to her but as her memory touches her heart, she realizes she knows this voice and turns sharply to see the Pigeon perched on a nearby branch looking down on them its wings outstretched and a glint in its eyes.

As the Witch's heart opens, all the energies of the forest around her fill the Witch's spirit. Tapping into the strength and love of the natural world surrounding her. From her heart, into her hands, she lifts clear the branch of the tree from the animal's body. With eyes wide and heart full, the Witch looks again into the deer's eyes as it stumbles to its feet. In its dark eyes, a reflection of the Pigeon beams back at the Witch. In that moment, the Witch realizes the power of friendship and love. Never far away if we look.

From that day on, the Witch determined to keep her heart open to all that needed it.

The Stone House

As the Witch enters through the small doorway into the stone house, she feels the cold of the house and a strange sensation as though the walls are vibrating. Sitting in the centre of the small space is a young woman. The space is so small that both women can barely fit in the room. The thick stone walls feel like they are closing in every day, but they afford protection and keep those inside safe from the outside. The Witch feels it difficult to breath in the small space and the coldness can be felt on the skin.

From the outside, nobody can see the young woman; a lot of the Villagers did not even know she still lived in the stone house. Others who did, said that nobody could help the young woman, only the woman could help herself and then only if she chose to.

The woman explained to the Witch how she could still remember laying the first brick of the stone house many months ago. The clay was made from her own sadness held together with tears. She could remember making the first bricks from her emotions after she sat holding her father's hand as he left his body behind for a better place.

There was a brick to represent the loss of her friend who had moved away and another brick for the passing of her dog who had died after many years of companionship. There was also a brick for the sorrow of a failed relationship and a sense of being alone. And yet another for the imagined hardships of others and the worry of events in the future not yet happened. She had cried so many tears.

For every upset in the woman's life, there was a brick added to the stone walls that now towered tall. The woman explained that after many months, she had become isolated inside the stone walls. She now felt she had no friends left and the stone walls kept new friends away. The vibration of the walls felt by the Witch on entering the house, was the woman's heart that was built into these walls in her sadness, now dulled, as past sorrows and regrets close in to be almost suffocating.

As the woman looks into the eyes of the Witch, she feels the tightness of her hand in hers and slowly, slowly, she feels the walls created of pain, fear and tears start to retreat. She begins to realize that past sorrows and mistakes are time points that we can choose to hold on to or choose to let go.

Life will always be complicated. Learn to be happy today before you run out of time and your self-built walls contain you.

The Voice Within.

The Witch knew that her mood had changed, and it was more than just the long dark evenings of Winter. The Witch felt as though an empty hole in her heart was growing bigger in some strange way.

She felt a sort of jealousy when she saw her brother the Simple Wizard McNnif with his partner Togram the Viking Woman even though she still could not understand her brother's attraction for the woman who measured female beauty by the size of her teeth. She bemoaned to herself that Viking women are just different and that her brother could do a lot better for himself.

Her friends, the Pigeon and the Frog, sensed the darkening mood of the Witch. But both felt powerless to influence this mood. The Pigeon wondered about how often we say we are ok or fine and hide behind a smile when people ask how we are. The Frog wondered how the world would be a different place if we took time to be less judgemental or if we could see the sadness, we each carry with us every day in our hearts.

The Witch falls to her knees emotionally weary at the kitchen floor. In that moment, she surrenders all sense of time and place. Through her teary eyes, she can hear music she has never heard before. It follows the rhythm of her tears falling to the kitchen flag stones and the beat of her heavy heart. The music comes from deep inside her and she feels it as strongly as anything she has felt before including her dislike for the Viking woman, Togram.

She focuses attention on the music that turns to a voice that the Witch has not heard in a long time. It is a voice from her childhood – and it draws closer as her concentration focuses more on the words spoken inside of her.

'Look up Witch. Open your eyes and look out to the night sky. The world seen through eyes filled with tears is very special for those who look'.

As the Witch looks up, she is amazed by the simple beauty of the world. It was as if the tears had cleaned the sparkle of the stars, the brightness of the moon, the beauty of the world as though she is seeing mother nature for the first time.

'It's the same sky that looks down on all of us' continued the inner voice. 'We all sleep under the same moon and take heat from the same sun, yet spend our time finding differences with others'.

The Pigeon coo'd softly. 'But why do we spend our time looking for differences between us?' it asks.

The Old Woman hesitates and then answers softly; 'We all have faults that we do not like, so we imagine those faults as belonging to others. It's much easier to see faults with others rather than see our own faults.

You can't clear your field while counting the rocks in your neighbours.

◆ ◆ ◆

Whispers of the Heart

In a small clearing, the Witch can see the tops of the trees glisten in the moon light. The night air is cold but there is a dryness tonight that is welcoming with a clear night sky alight with the stars. The Witch dressed in her long cape her arms part raised and palms facing towards the Moon. Her hair is blowing gently in the breeze. The Pigeon and the Frog take their respective places at the feet of the Witch. Like guard dogs but without the bite.

At the right moment, just as the Moon nears high point in the sky, the Witch commences her ceremony to the Moon Goddess. As she begins a rhythmic chant there is a strange quietness across the forest – even the owls have fallen silent. No other sound can be heard above the chanting of the Witch. 'Mistress of the night and of all magics, who rides the clouds in blackened skies, I pray by the Moon, I pray by the Moon, take me to the sky'.

The Pigeon and the Frog hold guard to their master as her mind journeys to other places across the sky to ensure that no one dares approach too close to the Witch in her travel state.

In her mind's eye, the Witch has arrived at a seashore and is standing looking out to a winter sea with breaking waves on a rocky shoreline. She feels the cold of the sea water as each wave rolls up the beach and surrounds her exposed feet. Never daring to expect anything during these magical journeys, she notices the approaching figure moving along the beach towards her. She can't help but to turn her attention to focus on the approaching figure loosely clothed in dark against the winter chill and cutting sea salt spray.

In the distance a loud roll of thunder momentarily distracts attention as it rolls across the sea and eventually disappears. Turning back, the Witch is for a moment startled by the closeness of the stranger, close enough so that she can feel his breath on her cheek. He lifts his head slowly to show his dark piercing eyes peering from under the hood of his cloak and speaks soft to her ear. 'Ask your question Witch'.

Holding her gaze to the roll of the waves, and after a brief pause, she responds. 'I had a dream that time was running dry like the sands in an hourglass. I saw life as a shooting star falling from the sky. In the morning, I woke so frightened to a bright dawn realizing all that I have already missed and the loved ones I have let go. Why we are not wise enough to give all that we are?'

Your Pride tells you it's not possible. Your Experience tells you it's too risky. Reason tells you it is pointless. If you love someone, you should let them know.

Listen to the whisper of your heart. It is telling you to give it a try. Try.

A Sad Pigeon

Over the last few days, the Pigeon is out of sorts and finding it hard to do anything. The Pigeon feels its heart heavy but does not know why.

To the annoyance of others, the Pigeon walks around the home pecking away at the legs of chairs out of boredom. Through a window, he can see outside and imagines the sun warming away the recent rain fall. Not feeling like going out, the Pigeon decides to perch down against the ground and just, well, 'Coo, Coo, Coo'

Disturbed by the Pigeon noise, the Frog jumps into sight. 'What's the matter with you Pigeon?' he cries out. The Pigeon doesn't answer and just scratches away at the stone floor. 'Heard you're not happy?' continued the small frog, tone softening.

'I just don't feel like doing much' the Pigeon eventually responds. 'I'm this way for a few days and don't know why' he coo'd.

The Frog stroked his chin and thought for a few seconds. 'Did the dream weavers visit you recently that perhaps disturbed your sleep?' he asked. 'No, I have not remembered my night journeys for some time now' responded the Pigeon in a dull flat tone. 'Frog, I know your only trying to help but I think I am beyond help today'. The Pigeon sniffed out loudly to himself. The Frog didn't know what to do and sat on his back legs for a minute pondering what to do next. The Frog thought to himself 'I need to get this Pigeon off it's back side and moving. Afterall, the happiest creatures are the ones that move about the most – maybe that's why the Pigeon is not happy'.

The Frog rolled up its tongue and with a quick flick unleashes it towards the bird's sleepy head smacking him just above his red eyeball. The Pigeon immediately responds with a flap of both wings – 'What did you do that for?' he shouts back to the Frog. 'I did that to get you moving off your sad ass. Let's go' cries the Frog and catching a hold of the Pigeon's wing drags the Pigeon out into the garden. A few feathers less, the Pigeon is flapping wildly in the garden, 'I don't want to go out' he protests. Next, the bird flops to the garden floor. 'Leave me' he sighs. After a few minutes silence, the bird feels soft hands cup his body and elevate him from the floor. As he opens his red eye, he sees the face of the Witch come closer. 'Sometimes we are busy with our own life to notice what is happening around us, but when our friends' heart is heavy, we feel it in our own hearts. It's like your dark cloud casts a shadow over all your friends' whispers the Witch into the face of the sad Pigeon.

Overhead a loud noise nears, and a flock of pigeons circles the Witch. Like a halo of birds around her moving with speed and a deafening sound of flapping and cooing. The Pigeon flaps his wings and joins them in their dance.

We don't always know why we feel sad, but there is always a way to find your smile. Sometimes, you just need to dance around for a while and your smile will find you.

Standing Ground.

'Speak Witch, what is the connection you have with this poop-machine Pigeon?' asks Togram the Viking Woman. 'It does nothing except eat and poop' she snarls through her broken teeth smile.

The Witch nods her head and after a short reflection tells the story of a chance meeting years ago. 'I grew up in a small village not far from here' she starts. 'When I was young, the other kids said that I was different from them. I don't know why, perhaps my long straw like hair or my simple black dress style. Maybe it was that I loved nature and brushing my teeth daily'.

The Witch went on to describe how she felt isolated and spent time on her own walking in the forest. She would fill her mind with question's like why the moon traversed the sky or marvel at how birds fly. The Witch recalled how this curiosity and her connection to Mother Nature and the Moon Goddess kept her occupied and stopped her thinking about those who didn't accept her.

She remembered when the village kids got bored and decided to pick on the her, pulling her hair and name calling. Maybe they were afraid of difference, or jealous of people who didn't blame others. At the start, the young Witch tried to plead with the ringleaders to leave her alone, but this seemed to have the opposite effect and encourage them more. One day, a group started calling the Witch cruel names and pulled her hair so hard that she broke away and ran from them as fast as possible so they would not see her tears. 'I ran into the dark forest where I knew they would not follow. I ran so hard that my heart pounded in my chest. I eventually stopped at a small clearance in the middle of the forest. There I came across the red-eye pigeon perched on a branch staring down at me. 'Leave me alone crazy bird!' she screamed at the Pigeon. 'Stop staring at me and just leave me be – you are just as bad as the others.' However, the Pigeon just kept staring and spoke softly. 'Dear Witch, we are nothing like those in your village. All we want is to be left in peace and live in harmony with Mother Nature. It is you who have come into our home and frightened our young.'

The Witch remembered thinking out loud to herself, 'I certainly didn't mean to frighten the young Pigeons, but these are just Pigeons who have no value and serve no real purpose as far as I can see'.

The Pigeon shook its head: 'For a Witch so gifted, you're not so clever when you are the target of other's ignorance.' With that, the Pigeon took to flight and left the Witch standing alone in the clearing surrounded by all of nature wild.

From that that day forward, the Witch chose to stand her ground in the face of ignorance and name calling. To stand up for the weaker and embrace difference. Her new confidence scared some away, but others learned to respect the Witch for who she is.

Some people will talk behind your back. Don't worry about it, they are behind you for a reason.

◆ ◆ ◆

The Voice Within.

That night, the Witch could not sleep and tossed and turned with thoughts running through her head until she had disturbed even the Pigeon. Outside, the sky is lit up with the splendid light of a full moon and stars that look like a thousand eyes blinking back. The Witch throws on her cape and resting the Pigeon on her shoulder, walks out into the night light.

After a short time, the Witch and her Pigeon come to the water's edge where she sees an old man crouched down staring at his reflection in the stillness of the water highlighted by the moon light. Without turning around, the old man welcomes the Witch and her Pigeon as though sensing their presence. "You are welcome to this place" he speaks in a deep tone.

The Witch responds softly 'My inner voice kept me awake, we could not sleep so decided to follow the light of the stars to come to this place. We are meaning you no disturbance and will go back to our place shortly'.

'No worries Witch, the Moon Goddess brought you to this place that we are here together at this time. These are the moments when we choose one path over another. Do you remember Witch when you faced life changing challenges in your past?'

'Yes, I remember them' responds the Witch softly.

'Well' speaks the old man, 'not everyone takes these challenges or faces up to the decisions we have to face in life. Some listen to their inner voice that grows arms and legs, and claws that holds our thoughts tightly. The voice flexes its claws just enough so that we can still see our dreams yet choke our souls to make us believe they are out of reach. This voice only speaks because we allow it and we feed and keep it alive inside'.

'Yes, I hear this inner voice that tells me what I can and can't do' responds the Witch listening intently.

The old man continues. 'Do not worry Witch. The voice does not haunt you alone. The strongest warrior, the wisest, the kindest, the bravest, all take visitation from this inner voice. The story is always different for each of us. But it can be defeated'.

'Question every fear that rises inside you – check for truths and eventually you will see a pattern. You will find that negative thoughts are just thoughts that can be dismissed by choice. You will find that new situations may be wonderful and full of opportunity'.

We only regret the chances we do not take.

CATCH A DREAM

Stories are very special and older than science and even FrogSnap. In the past, it was the telling of stories that helped to pass on life lessons and help others to be the best they can. However, stories are just one of three aspects in life that connect the past, the present and the future. 'Besides stories, what are the other two aspects that connect across the past, the present and the future?' wondered the Witch out loud.

'Dreams' answered the Pigeon almost indignantly as though stating the obvious.

'And Imagination' croaked in the Frog Robert.

'It is your dreams' the Pigeon explains 'that connects a time in your past to a point in the future that has not yet happened. Everyone experiences dreams of a time in the past when we were hurt or upset or scared. Usually, when we are most frightened and in trouble in the dream, like falling or when we are surrounded by shadows that creates a sense of fear, we awake startled, sweaty, even crying out in the night. But if we could stay in our dream and not wake, we may find that dreams can also provide answers to questions that we ask. Sometime, people awake from dreams feeling refreshed and a new sense of purpose with an answer to a question that may have troubled them recently'.

The Frog interrupts the Pigeon with a snap of it's tongue.

'Dreams can also warn us about what is about to happen in your life, who you might meet and how you might react to them. Sometimes we dream about someone we love or care about and then find yourself bumping into them soon afterwards – these are the dreams I love the best' croaks the frog.

'What about day dreams?' asks the Witch thinking of the times when she sat staring out through the window at the movement of trees in the wind or gazing up at the stars on a bright night sky.

The Pigeon continued. 'They are the same Witch, they bring us to places we need to go, or they help to remind us of people we have forgotten. At its simplest, day dreams are an escape from the troubles of the day and can help us to see what is truly important in our lives'.

'Imagination is like awake dreaming and is magic when experienced with awareness. Think about a child's expression as their eyes follow a butterfly, or a cloud or a cat chase its own shadow. Or a time when you appreciated beauty in art or nature or music or felt the warmth of connection holding the hand of someone you care about. That is real magic, that's the moment you can feel magic. It's when you call someone, and they cannot hear because they are lost in the beauty of their imagination'.

Always believe in yourself. Your dreams can come true and it is in your dreams that you see the truth of who you are meant to be. The Witch was beginning to understand more clearly. 'But how will I know if I am living the best life I can?' she asks.

'There are two things to remember. Firstly, in life you make choices that allow your greatest dreams to come true. And secondly, we are happiest in life when we follow the path that is closest to our imagination,' beamed the Pigeon.

The Frog Hop.

'Do you want to dance?' booms a deep voice over the blaring music. The Witch looks up from her phone startled, and surprised that someone would cross the dance floor to ask her to dance. Without thinking too much about it, she places her hand to his and stands up to look into the face of Robert. Taking her hand gently in his, he leads her to the centre of the dance floor through the steaming crowd of dancers moving slowly to the beat of the music. She feels his strong arms around her waist, and he pulls her closer. His scent is familiar. The Witch blushes not used to someone else taking control of her in this way.

'You've been away awhile' she shouts to his ear 'looks like you got a bit of a colour too'. Robert adjusts his head slightly so he can respond. 'Surprised that you noticed – I've been close all the while' he speaks through the Witch's hair so that she can hear.

The Witch is still slightly flustered with the close contact between the two but recognising the familiarity existing between them still. In that moment the pair drift along to the music and flashing lights. Aware of the presence of others around her, in her mind she wishes they were somewhere else. Robert looks to her eyes as though hearing her thoughts. The background fades suddenly and the music dies away. Closing her eyes when she opens them again, they are no longer at the village dance and instead standing alone in a lighting storm at some distant place.

Robert releases the Witch from his gentle hold and steps back looking to the sky as though suddenly aware of change in surroundings. Looking back to the Witch standing before him recognizing her inner strength and at the same time her vulnerability. Her wild hair blowing in the wind creates a perfect halo contrasting with the lightning in the black sky behind her as though painted in flames. 'We should return' she whispers over the wind reaching her hand forward towards Robert.

'Not yet Witch' Robert interjects over the storm. 'What if this storm ends and leaves us with nothing except a distant echo of memories?'. Just then a silver fork strike lights the sky behind, silhouetting the Witch, creating a perfect halo of golden hair and lightning. The Witch is radiating. Her hair is charged with the static from the storm lifting it from her shoulders making it look wild in the wind.

Reaching both her hands towards him, she takes his hands in hers. In that instant they are back at the Frogs Hop in the midst of the music and flashing lights. It takes a second to adjust back to the surroundings. Opening her eyes, she sees that Robert is standing before her. They are surrounded by dancers stepping from one foot to the other like a native dance routine developed for frogs on hot plates.

You can't start the next chapter in your life, if you keep re-reading the last one.

◆ ◆ ◆

Never Black & White

Long, long ago, before Instagram and even Facebook, there lived a beautiful princess. The princess was the youngest of long line of fairy folk and was next in line to be queen of the fairies. From a young age, the fairy princess was showered with gifts and compliments on her beauty. She was big into fashion and with her online phone she followed the latest trends and strange beauty practices from the tribes across the great seas that could be delivered to her door.

Although she was happy, the fairy princess yearned for more and it became very difficult to please the princess. Her friends and family became so frustrated with the princess hoping that she would eventually grow out of her obsession. However, as the princess became older and started dating, she still could not find happiness.

Every time she met someone new, she would expect the impossible from them. And each time she would blame her boyfriend for the demise of their romance. Sometimes, they would be frightened away by her expectations of fancy jewels, clothing and holiday destinations promoted by pictures of various on-line social media platforms by those who made look like a photograph posted on-line.

And every time a romance crumbled, the princess lost a little more of herself. Those closest to the princess began to recognize that the once pure soul was lost to impossible expectations falsely portrayed through online media. Essentially, she was mastering her own ugly destiny.

She had everything anyone could ever wish for, yet it was never enough compared to the fantastic lives portrayed by the on-line bloggers she followed on-line.

After a while, the Princess started to fear her failed relationships might be because she was not beautiful enough. So, again searching the internet, she started buying so called magic potions to change her appearance, to change her skin tone, or make her eyes wider or highlight her hair colour. The only thing that stayed the same was monthly subscriptions paid to on-line dating sites that everyone knows are for life and cannot be cancelled.

Eventually, the princess became isolated from her friends who had also enough of her vanity. She moved to a small village with limited internet access and it is said that the only company she had was a Pigeon and a Frog. It is even rumoured by some that the princess spent long days talking to the Pigeon or the Frog believing they could talk back to her.

Nobody really knows what happened to the fairy princess – except that her suitors eventually stopped coming as a fear grew of the princess and her high expectations.

Anyway, lifting her cup from the table, the Witch sips her tea loudly. Alone, again, except for the presence of the Pigeon and the Frog. 'We are masters of illusion as we shelter our desires'. The

Pigeon, her dearest companion responds as it only can, 'Coo.... Coo....'

Everything that comes to you starts with how you feel about yourself. Start there first.

CHOICES

On the way to the Park for coffee, the Witch and her Pigeon decide to take a shortcut through the forest. Sun light coming through the trees fills the Witch with new hope for the coming season. As they approach the edge of the clearing the path diverges in front of them. At the beginning, both paths appear the same but looking into the future as far as the Witch could, she realized that each path could bring them on a very different journey. However, the Witch could not see so far into the future to tell if each path would lead to a different place and time. One of the paths looked more familiar than the other and had a clear path line as though trodden by many others before her.

The second path looked more challenging. The pathway appeared to be rough and looked overgrown in some places. The signs were unusual, and they all pointed to new and different experiences. The Witch thought for a minute about her choices and realizing that she would need to make the decision soon before fading light brought them to darkness in the forest. The Pigeon was comfortable in the Witch's pocket and decided to stay quiet for the moment.

The Witch knew that she had three options: make a choice, stay where she was or go back the same way. The fear of making the wrong choice troubled the young Witch as equal as making no choice. It was as if the Witch was stuck in the moment of indecision. The Witch reached to her cape pocket and gently lifted the

Pigeon to her hand. 'Two paths diverge' she whispers to the dozing Pigeon. 'Which one should I follow?'.

The Pigeon blinks its eyeballs and twitches nervously. 'Should is the wrong word. Others will tell you the road you should follow but only you can choose the road to take'.

The Witch looked down both paths as far as she could. 'But how will I know if I am making the right choice?' she thought out loud.

'Your heart will know'

'And if I am wrong?'

'If you are wrong, you can always make another choice. Life is about choices and every choice you make makes who you are.

The Witch closed her eyes and began to pray to Mother Earth for guidance in her path choice.

When the Witch opened her eyes again, she saw a large Stag standing in the clearing some way down one of the path ways. The Stag was majestic and still. It reminded the Witch of someone she had not thought about for a long time. She remembered the voice of her grandfather before he had passed. 'Your guardian angel is always with you and takes many forms and shapes, if only you have the eyes to see and ears to hear'.

The Witch stood up and began to journey onwards. She knew which path to follow and so will you.

Cunning Pigeon

The Pigeon's belly grumbled at him, nagging him to find something to eat. The local villagers are not fond of pigeons unless on a dinner plate and scraps of food for Pigeons are not plentiful.

The Pigeon shrugged its shoulders and thought perhaps he just had it too easy for too long at the Witches house taking food whenever he needed. As the Pigeon approached the coop he spots the Frog snoozing on a rock beside the pond. The Pigeon swoops down and lands beside the Frog. 'Poor Pigeon' croaks the Frog, 'are you very hungry?'. The Pigeon nods and coo's softly in a sympathetic tone.

'Speak to me, brother Pigeon,' said the Frog gently throwing its tongue to touch the Pigeons beak. The Pigeon said nothing but sank to the floor with a sigh. The Frog was getting slightly worried now and nudged the Pigeon every so often trying to provoke a response from the normally cranky bird. 'You look a little thin' croaks the Frog 'are you really so hungry?' Again, there is no response from the Pigeon.

The Frog hops into the darkness and reappears a few moments later with a swollen mouth full of seeds. Placing the seeds at the feet of the Pigeon. The Pigeon blinks its eyeball and gobbles away the food quickly. 'Is that better?' asks the Frog. The Pigeon makes a small effort of trying to nod his head but seems too weak to lift his head. The Frog hopped away again into the night and returned a few minutes later with his mouth expanded like a football. He spewed the seeds and nuts out in front of the Pigeon. This exercise was repeated a number of times during the night where the Frog leaped off into the woods returning with his mouth expanded full of nuts, seeds and grains. By the end of that night, the Pigeon had consumed a barrel load. 'Brother Pigeon' asked the Frog peering closely at the grey / blue Pigeon, 'can you fly? You should not be here in daylight when the cat from next door makes its morning appearance'. The Pigeon pretended to flap its wings 'I'm not sure I can move', he spoke quietly. 'Thank you for all your help, leave me here and go off to the safety of your smelly pond'.

The Frog was worried now and extended his webbed foot so that he could place it around the Pigeon. The Frog carried and drags the Pigeon and eventually gets the Pigeon back to his Pigeon Coop. For almost a full moon phase, the Pigeon lazed about, with the Frog bringing it food nightly from the forest. Then one evening, the Pigeon decided he'd had enough of dry food brought by the Frog and made his way into the sky to dine on the farmers newly planted seeds. On the way back he spots the Frog down on its rock beside the pond. The Pigeon swoops down beside the Frog. 'You look a little pale yourself tonight Frog' coos the Pigeon with a smirk across his beaky face. 'How could you?' croaked the frog. With that the Pigeon took airborne and flew back to its Pigeon Coop.

To this day, Pigeons are known to be cunning creatures and Frogs have learned to be, well, they have learned to be just Frogs.

◆ ◆ ◆

Your World or Mine

'Darksome Night and Shining Moon, East then South, then West then North' starts the Witch as she prepares to cast her circle. She is surrounded by the villagers who are by-standers in this process recognizing that the power is with the small person at the centre of an imaginary circle. 'Earth and Water, Wind and Fire...' continues the Witch. Overhead, the clouds darken to black, and the wind is rising. If you look to the sky now you will see it.

The Witch stands at the centre of the circle with her arms outstretched to the sky holding conversation with an invisible force above her in the sky. On the ground beside her, the trusted Pigeon holds its own ceremony as it steps from one foot to the other as though on hot stones.

The group of on-lookers are becoming restless amidst a growing muttering of impatience getting louder. The Witch has sensed the unease around her from the uninvited spectators and slowly bringing her arms to her side brings her attention to the crowd. These are mostly settled Vikings who have turned to farming or fishing for their livelihood. 'Who wants to ask the Moon Goddess favour?' calls out the Witch in a shrill voice over the wind to a crowd who have now fallen silent as the attention has moved to them.

Following a short moment of silence – a young Viking man steps forward. Tall and still strong, the man approaches confidently towards the Witch. The Pigeon places itself to act as the distance marker between his master and guest. The Witch has watched the tall man approach and now has eye contact. She notices the sharp lines of the man's face and the deepness of his eyes that appear as sad as a mountain lake. 'Speak boy – what do you counsel in the presence of the Moon Goddess?'

'I am of youth, that you will soon forget Witch' he speaks in a strong tone. 'Don't you feel lonely living in your own little world?'

The sky suddenly closes in around the pair standing on this hill top and time has stopped for everyone except the Witch and the Viking man. She steps forward and takes his hands in hers that he accepts willingly. The wind is sweeping around them forming a vortex of silence around the pair as though to isolate them from the world. Leaning towards the young man, the Witch touches her soft face to his rough and whispers to his ear. 'Don't your feel powerless living in other people's worlds?'

Drawing back from the man – the Witch steps back into the circle. The sky lifts from the pair and the surrounding comes back into focus. The man lifts his face and smiles an acknowledgement back to the Witch. 'I have heard the Moon Goddess'.

People with a good sense of humour have a better sense of life.

Dawning.

The Witch is sat in her garden feeling the strength of the ground beneath her body, always constant. Eyes closed she soaks up the sun just glad to have the quiet time to herself to marvel at the beauty of a late spring evening. At her cloak tails is the dozing Pigeon and the Frog. Cooing and Croaking in a rythmic pattern like a new version of hip hop.

Just then, the Witch hears a car pull up in front of the house. Wishing it was not so, the Viking Woman arrives at the front door. The Witch wonders for a moment if the front door is locked and perhaps, she might just drive on. However, that thought disappears quickly as the burly Viking woman lets herself in and thunders through into the kitchen and out into the garden. 'Witch, I was bored and decided to pay you a visit in case you're not' calls the Viking with her head bopping from side to side. 'Oh good' responds the Witch, slightly sarcastic; 'have you done something with your hair recently, I see you went for the rats nest style' The Viking grins widely through her broken teeth like the front grill of a tractor. 'A rain shower is forecast, and I am on my way with the Village folk to see if we can find the gold at the end of the rainbow and wondered if you wanted to join us?' she asks.

The Witch seizes the opportunity and tells the Viking she's busy with counting tea bags and wishes them all success. The Viking woman leaves shortly back to her car outside.

Watching the fleet of cars and vans drive away into the distance, the Witch thinks how sad it must be for those who spend their lives in the pursuit of false promises, waiting for a tomorrow that might never come. Of course, the real beauty of the rainbow was not to be found somewhere over the rainbow or at the end of the rainbow but was here, now, under the rainbow.

Perhaps the world is a creation of how we choose to see it. Its as simple as opening our eyes and looking at all we have in our life. Moments pass and with them opportunities if we let them.

The Witch, the Pigeon and the Frog suddenly felt a sadness for the people who make the greatest mistake of their life following the dreams of others. Perhaps they have not yet learned that every person can find their own treasure but to do so means following your own path that is true to your own dream.

Sometimes we forget from where the sun will rise. But it always dawns on us... eventually.

GHOST IN THE FOG

The 3 am darkness is disturbed by unexpected sounds from downstairs. It sounds like voices although there is no one else in the house except the Pigeon and the Frog. The Witch listens more intently – perhaps a dream she thinks to herself. Nope, she hears the muffled voices again and jumps to her feet. The Witch makes her way quietly down the stairs to the kitchen door hoping to frighten off the night visitor. A Witch in a night dress with staff in hand is still a formidable sight that should not be taken lightly.

The Witch creeps towards the closed kitchen door pushing her wild hair aside from her ear leaning into the door. Listening intently, she hears muffled voices.

The next sound is familiar to the Witch as she hears the cooing of the Pigeon that sounds in panic. Opening the kitchen door, the Witch peers into a moonlit incense filled kitchen and sees the Pigeon on the table but no one else. The Pigeon blinks wildly but hard to tell if this is more than normal Pigeon twitch.

Scanning the room quickly the Witch can see no one else. 'Who are you talking to Pigeon?' she asks cowering over the blinking Pigeon. Suddenly, a voice starts up again, causing the Witch to reflexively stand straight with the long staff in front of her, defensively.

Seeing no one else and with zero martial arts training, she has adopted a stance that any Ninja would be proud of! 'Show your-self, who ever you are' cries out the Witch turning slowly but eventually back to the Pigeon that is nodding its head back and forth towards a silver box on the table. The Witch lifts the lid slowly and from it rises a white fog that quickly fills the small room. The Witch backs up against the door, not in fear, but an-ticipation for what might come next. The moonlight through the back window is sending beams through the fog filled kitchen like a dancefloor spotlight with invisible dancers.

Then, from the white fog two outstretched arms reaching to-wards the Witch who is now shaking with growing fear. 'Take my hands, Witch' commands a strong voice from the white dense fog. Her mind is momentarily paralysed, and she drops the staff reach-ing forward to take both hands in her hers. In that moment, the stranger pulls her forward and she is scooped up into strong arms. Feeling the rush of a strong safe embrace, her heart races. In sec-onds, the Witch feels the cool night air as she is lifted skywards against a strong downdraft and a loud roar overhead. This must be the night Hunter come to take me, she thinks to herself. Or... the rescue helicopter is up?

Some people search a long time to find the truth of who they are meant to be. Many make this mistake, searching far and wide to find themselves. Others realize that what they seek is not an out-ward journey but an inward reflection to find their true self. Who looks outside, dreams. Who looks inside, awakens.

The Elevator Pitch.

The elevator doors open and the Witch with her Frog in pocket and Pigeon on her forearm step into the empty elevator. Its one of those changing room size elevators with lounge music piped in via a ceiling mounted speaker. The Witch Presses the key pad for top floor room 33.

As the elevator moves upwards the Witch thinks to herself that at least we don't have to share with a stranger – that would be awkward. This thought is momentary though as the bell sounds – 'bing'- and the elevator slows to a stop at the 10th floor. The Witch moves to the back of the elevator as the new passenger steps in. 'Going down?' inquires the passenger as she looks the Witch up and down. 'Emm… no we are going up' speaks the Witch in a hopeful tone. As though not listening, the passenger responds 'Good' and presses the door close button and the journey upwards recommences.

Inside the elevator, the passenger is a very tall woman dressed all in black and the Witch wonders if she is perhaps hotel staff – a porter or house-keeping. 'Bing' that now familiar sound and the elevator draws to a stop at 21.

As the door opens – a girl with a gigantic vacuum cleaner is standing at the door and gestures towards the open door with the suction nozzle. Just as she is about to step forward, the tall passenger raises one hand to the girl and closes the door with the other. The Witch is surprised by the rude action of the passenger. 'Excuse me' speaks the Witch 'there was no need for that rudeness'. The passenger pushes herself off the leaning rail to stand up right to look down on the Witch. Crikey – this is a big woman, thinks the Witch who is looking up at this giant of a woman silhouetted by the roof fluorescent lighting.

'You should not have a Pigeon in an elevator' speaks the passenger in a menacing tone. The Passenger has adopted a stance not unfamiliar to a rugby back line. The Witch registering the threat calmly lifts the frog from her pocket and holds it out on her outstretched left palm. Looking surprised, the passenger bends forward to better see the small green creature. As the woman's face nears the small frog the Witch leans to meet the woman's ear and speaks.

'How people behave towards others, is a direct reflection of how they feel about themselves'.

The mysterious passenger recoils and stands square. After reciting what sounds like a number sequence, the tall passenger suddenly vanishes from the small confined space leaving nothing but a scorch mark on the floor and ceiling of the elevator. The next sound is that bell – 'ding'. The doors open and the indicator reads 33.

Do the best that you can in the place that you are. Being kind to others is a small effort that says a lot about who you are.

◆ ◆ ◆

Classy Bird

'Are you ready?' asks the Witch looking intently at the Pigeon. 'I seem to be always waiting on you bird'. The Pigeon is blinking as though pondering its response. 'We are different yet so much the same' continues the Witch as she cups her hands gently around the bird. Bringing the bird closer to her face, she stares intently at the Pigeon who is doing its best not to make direct eye contact. 'We can do anything if we put our minds to it, just give me your heart' she speaks softly to the bird, 'tonight we will be as one'.

The next sensation is of wind and rain as the Pigeon as the Witch are in flight. The Witch feels her heart beating so quickly and notices how small lungs struggle to catch breath in the night sky as she fly's as a bird through the rooftops towards the river. The rain is making the effort of flight more difficult and eventually the Pigeon sets down on the tall mast of a river boat moored along the bank. Summer rain showers are different than the cold winter showers of past months. The Witch believes that the summer rain washes away past regrets and signals the passing of the grey days of winter with a new hope for the future and what can be.

Watching below, a couple holding hands walk by indifferent to the rain, their mission to get somewhere preoccupying them. A sudden sadness takes hold of the bird as a sense of lost opportunity envelops the small creature. The Pigeon's mind is suddenly racing as emotions take hold. With a flutter of wings, the bird descends to the ground and the Witch reforms feeling the ground once more beneath her feet. As the Witch surveys her location she realizes that she is not alone, and another human form is approaching her with intent. To her left side, the large shape of a burley Viking is approaching quickly – he calls out to the Witch, but his language is not fully heard over the rain. As he nears, his intent is a now a genuine concern as he raises one arm above his head like a salute. The small demeanour of the Witch is no physical threat to these Vikings who are sea warriors that have recently settled in the Village to learn new ways of farming and live a peaceful existence. For most of the time anyway.

'State your intention' calls out the Witch nervously still spitting pigeon feathers. Not registering the instruction, or perhaps not understanding the meaning, the Viking continues his path trajectory towards the Witch. Raising her arms to the sky the Witch prepares to spell cast the Viking or change form back to the Pigeon. But it is too late. In that moment, the Viking has reached her, and she feels strong arms around her pulling her in. 'You're a classy bird' mumbles the Viking through his bearded face. 'Come out with me woman and you will be eating frogs not pigeon'.

New experience can be scary. Set your fears aside. Either it will work out, or it won't. That's just life.

Remember that hope dances in the puddles until the sun comes out again.

The Shopping Aisle Encounter

Pushing the shopping trolley down the dry foods aisle the Witch is not thinking beyond what she will have for tea. The supermarket is its usual busy with some just cruising the shopping aisles as though searching for something lost. As the Witch rounds the corner heading to the fruit and veg aisle, she recognises the Viking Woman, Togram.

The Witch makes a sharp turn in the opposite direction in the hope to avoid the Viking Woman, taking her trolley sharply into the pet food section. 'OMG – that was a close call' says the Witch leaning into the Pigeon. The Pigeon is perched up on the frame of the trolley but has perked up since entering the pet food section. 'Alright, alright, let's not get over excited bird, we are just here to avoid the Viking woman', speaks the Witch to dampen the rising excitement of the Pigeon. Maybe animal instinct, but the Pigeon senses that there is easy food here nearby and is flapping to show its raised interest. 'Bird, please don't embarrass me, calm down' calls the Witch hoping to settle the flapping bird. Just then a thundering voice calls out 'Hello Witch, Hello you'. It's the Viking woman Togram who having seen the Witch is now bearing down on the Witch's trolley position.

'How nice to see you' starts Togram through her broken teeth smile. 'I thought it was you when I heard your Pigeon flapping' she continues. The Witch gives the Pigeon a scathing glance before turning her forced smile back to Togram. 'Oh. hi, what a lovely surprise to see you here!' responds the Witch as she recoils slightly from the strong Viking eau de parfume. 'So, what brings the Wicked Witch of the North in here?' continues the Viking Togram in a sarcastic tone. 'Well, I thought I'd just pick up something light for the tea' responds the Witch.

'Sure, sure' continues Togram grabbing hold of the Witch's shopping trolley. 'But your looking so well since I've seen you last. The black works on you so well'. The Witch tries to move her trolley hoping that the Viking Woman might move on in a different direction. However, the strength of the Viking woman holds firm. 'Still shopping for one I see?' exclaims the Viking Woman with apparent glee as she peers into the shopping trolley of the Witch. The Witch stops wrestling the trolley and turns towards the face of the Viking Woman. Togram looks into the eyes of the Witch and sees a sadness in them that she had not noticed before. She realizes that people hide true feelings and to never judge a book by its cover.

Leaning to the Witch's ear, she whispers. 'Someday Witch, you will meet eyes with someone who makes you feel at home with the world and you will think to yourself. Ah, there you are...'

Door Canvasing

'Can someone please get the door' cries out the Witch as though forgetting she's home alone with a Pigeon and a Frog. Making a growling noise, the Witch eventually presses pause on the TV and jumps to her feet to open the front door. As the door swings open, the Witch is greeted by a young man in a suit with leaflets in hand outstretched offering a gift to the unsuspecting. 'What do you want'? roars the Witch to the suited man at the door.

The man steps forward with his leaflet extended toward the Witch in the part open doorway. 'Hello, I'm from the local Frog election party and wondered if we could have a few minutes to explain our policies?' The Witch is taken aback with the young man's arrogance. Growling back at the young man, the Witch scans him up and down noticing his black patent shoes and smart shirt to his beaming smile with a perfect row of teeth that suggests serious cosmetic whitening. No one's teeth naturally gleam like that she thinks to herself.

Holding one hand on the door ready to slam it shut, she extends the other forward and takes the information leaflet from the young man. Smiling back at him, 'I'll read it later and thanks for calling'. With that she steps back into the hall and starts to close the door on the visitors. As she does, the door unexpectedly catches an obstruction that prevents the door from moving. Glancing down the Witch is surprised to see a shoe in the door jamb that prevents the door from closing. Swinging the door back open – the Witch looks to the man who is still smiling through his gleaming teeth. 'Eh... what are you doing? If you don't remove your foot, there will be consequences' she roars into his face. Not flinching, the young man, holds his position. 'Can I count on your vote?' he counters back to the Witch. The Witch feels tension rise inside her as she purses her lips tight as though sucking air through a straw.

Like from a Clint Eastwood movie, the Witch steps down from the doorstep and stands square to the suited man who is now slightly taller looking. Looking up at his youthful face she wonders who this person is that challenges a Witch on her home ground. The man's facial expression changes and the wide beaming smile starts to slowly subside as he feels the uncomfortable closeness of the Witch to his face. She is close enough now to smell his aftershave and feel his heat. For just a moment, the Witch feels the young mans heart beating a nervous rhythm before a voice from within the house shouts out over them 'shut the front door' that jolts her back to the present moment and makes her recoil from the young man's face.

'Sounds like someone is having a bad day' retorts the young man gesturing with his head towards the open door.

The Witch peers back – 'Life isn't about having a good day or a bad day or waiting for the storm to pass. It's about learning to dance in the rain'.

You are always only one decision away from a totally different life.

DANCING BY
THE RIVER

The Witch's path is lit by starlight in the dark sky. Her companions, the Pigeon and the Frog are hold up in the Witch's deep cloak pockets and content to do so on this dark night journey to the Witch's tribal home.

As the Witch crosses the river the thick mist parts and the three ship banners of the Deise Tribe comes into view. Next to the river, a large pavilion is standing and the blue and white of the banners are flying in the breeze. The music is much louder now. It's a traditional music played on pipes and fiddles with drumbeats that follow their own rhythm. Dancing figures can be made out on the water's edge. Most seem to be naked, or nearly so, with glances of light on their skin from the small crescent moon overhead. The dancing is wild with most just writhing to the drumbeats. The dancers are splashing in and out of the dark water that has a vale of mist just above its surface that offers some coverage to the partially naked dancers. The sound of loud laughing mixed with yelps and part screams from the revellers fills the night.

As the Witch approaches the central pavilion they enter through the curtan entrance to a large covered space. Inside, the Deise chiefs are gathered seated around a large circular table of oak. A hand is raised by one of the chieftains to signal to the Witch to take her seat at the table. 'So, you have arrived' he calls out to the young Witch. The Witch takes her place at the table. Feeling movement in her cloak pocket, the Witch reaches inside and places the Pigeon on the table in front of her. A gentle pat to the other pocket to settle the Frog who must stay in his pocket hideaway for another while.

'Begin' booms a voice from the top of the large table. Each seated, places both hands flat on the table. 'Chords and Sensor, Scourge and Knife, by all the power of the blade, here I come to call thee forth' begins the chant around the table. Behind her, the Witch can feel the presence of wisps or ghostly figures of those that have lost someone or something. They whisper loudly holding multiple conversations at the same time to make the voices indiscernible to those not supposed to hear.

In her minds' eye, the Witch sees the approach of a large stag, the earthly form of the horned hunter. Flaring its nostrils, the animal claws a hoof against the rough ground signalling its presence to those that see. In this dream state, the Witch reaches forward to gently touch the shoulder of the animal. The Witch feels the power of the animal through the palm of her hand. It is the power of Mother Earth. Raw, yet gentle.

A voice whispers in the Witch's mind. 'Learn to love the sound of your feet walking away from what is not meant for you'.

The Witch's focus comes back to the room. The Pigeon Coo's and the Frog stirs restlessly in her pocket.

Speed Dating a Witch

As the game begins, the first candidate for the Witch is a solid looking farmer with teeth not out of place in a horse. He extends his hand and offers a clammy hand shake to the Witch. 'So, what's your name?' asks the farmer nervously of the Witch. 'Witch is good' is the curt response with her head tilted to one side. 'And what do you do for a living?' he gingerly presses on. 'Well I'm not a plumber' is the sarcastic response from across the table. The farmer man looks down at his prepared list of questions losing his practiced train of thought.

'Is that your own hair?' he stutters out at the Witch. With that, the buzzer sounds, and the man stands to his feet shaking his head to move to the next candidate. The next participant sitting opposite the Witch is a butch looking Viking with wild eyebrows and what looks like potatoes growing from his ears. 'Hi, my name is Rodriquez' he speaks with some anticipation in his voice. The Witch looks at him for a second as though waiting for the next sentence. 'Really' she responds eventually, 'that is unfortunate'. As the time buzzer sounds, the rotation of candidates continues but there is little improvement on the social skills or interest level from the Witch. Focusing her attention on her long nails during the next interview, the Witch is struggling to maintain more than a passing interest on the revolving suiters.

After ten minutes that feel like the tide has gone out, the Witch is confronted by the final participant. The Witch is already looking out vacantly past the seated man looking to the door wondering if there will be tea and refreshments post event. There is always a rush on the ginger nuts she thinks to herself and usually gone quickly.

The Witch is suddenly startled back into the present moment as she feels a light touch on her arm from the presence opposite. Recoiling her arm quickly, she looks at the face of the man opposite. 'Don't touch me dude' she spits back into his face before even registering him. 'Thought your mind was far away' responds the man in a soft voice tone that is not typical in this area. The Witch now looks the man up and down as though examining a pork chop at the butchers. 'What do you see in my eyes?' continues the soft tone voice. The Witch is surprised at his question and instinctively looks into the man's deep eyes. 'I see troubled water' responds the Witch without thinking. The man nods to the Witch and responds, 'I see the moon in yours'. There is a moment of silence between the two that somehow connects them across the small wooden table cancelling out the background noise of meaningless chatter around the room. The next words spoken between the pair are not heard. For in that moment, the Witch feels emotions not felt in a long time. The man places his hand back on the Witch's forearm. This time she does not recoil. Leaning towards her across the table he whispers. 'You are like a feather. Strong with purpose yet light at heart. We all become frayed but always able to pull it back together.'

If you never try, you'll never know.

Don't Call Me Robert.

Back in the old days, like before 2001, it was usual to bring the new fella round to meet the family. Since then, things have not changed much. The Witch has brought the new man in her life round for Sunday dinner to meet hers, the Pigeon and the Frog.

The Pigeon is on the table partaking in the occasion in its own way although on a separate vegan menu of corn. The Frog is also present on the table in his water bowl listening intently to the conversation.

'What's the story with the Pigeon and Frog on the table?' asks the dinner guest. 'They are friends' answers the Witch in a definitive tone. 'Really?' continues the new boyfriend, eager to show interest in the Witch's pets. 'Pigeons are such messy creatures' he continues. The Pigeon's attention rises, and its eyes are darting around in its little head as though trying to escape. 'I heard that the last fella didn't last long' continues the inquisitive guest in a casual tone. 'Someone called Robert or Roberto I hear' he continues ignoring the increasing agitation of the Pigeon and the Frog. The Witch, trying to deflect the conversation interjects, 'they are great company since my sister had her accident with a washing machine last year. At least I know she passed in comfort'. The guest doesn't react to the Witch's diversionary tactic and is still focused on the agitated bird.

'Calm yourself bird' he says, 'everyone knows you're here'. The guest smiles broadly at the silencing of the pesky bird on the table. 'I was asking about your last boyfriend?' continues the guest 'before the bird got excited'.

The Witch throws a quick look to her guest. 'Let's not go there' she speaks, 'the past should stay in the past'. The Frog is now paddling furiously in the water dish as though practicing the breast-stroke for the next Olympics. The guest leans closer to the small amphibious creature on the table. 'What is wrong with this Frog?' He asks with word emphasis. 'He doesn't like it much when you mention the ex-boyfriend' speaks the Witch gingerly with a head tilt as though slightly awkward on the topic. 'Anyway, his name wasn't Robert'. The guest has a slightly confused look on his face moves closer to the Frogs dish, his eyeballs fully exposed. 'What was his name then?' persists the guest peering closer down onto the Frog.

In an instant there is a sharp crack and the Frog has launched its tongue directly into one of the eyeballs in the sky – the guest recoils with the pain holding both hands over his left eye. 'What the flip was that' roars the guest, momentarily losing his cool demeanour shown to date. As though rebounding from a boxing punch, he leans back towards the Frog who has now climbed to the edge of the water bowl and is in a demented rant. Ribbet, Ribbet, Ribbet, Ribbet.

'See, I told you his name wasn't Robert' muses the Witch.

The Pigeon flaps in contentment. Everyone must experience the dark to appreciate the light.

Hanging by the Phone

The Frog and The Pigeon are less than happy. Frog's water bowl is murky and resembles an algae infested pond with each passing day. The Witch is watching Love Island back to back and has heard nothing from her new man since the Frog tasted the mans eyeball.

The Pigeon longs to stretch its wings in the fresh outdoors. Both make a beeline for the door glancing hopefully at the Witch. "NO!" she roars, "No one goes outside until I'm ready!" She hurls a takeaway carton at the door in frustration, causing an indignant croak and squawk. The Pigeon zips out of the room and the Frog leaps under an armchair eyeing the Witch with dissent. "What?!" she snaps, glaring at The Frog. "This is your fault, if you hadn't licked my date none of this would be happening." The Frog hops out of the room while the Witch moodily settles back into her nest of blankets, her body imprinted onto the couch.

Rain patters along the roof that grows louder and faster by the minute. "See?" mutters the Witch, at no one in particular, "it's raining anyways." The Witch glances at her phone every five minutes double checking she hasn't missed a call or text. She turns her data on and off just in case it's not working. It's a week and she still hasn't heard anything from the man, growing more embarrassed with every passing day. She knows she should really call to apologise about the incident with the Frog, but it's hardly her fault.

She wishes she had made the Frog and Pigeon eat separately from them. They can be such a nuisance, especially to her dating life. "Maybe I'd be better off without them" muses the old Witch.

Hours pass, absolutely nothing has happened on Love Island, and the Witch hasn't move from the couch. After a while an ad pops up. It's the one with a pigeon in it advertising for cards – dopey pigeon or funky frog or something.com. Anyway, they always get a great hoot out of it.

"Look guys - your cousin is on tv!" exclaims the Witch automatically looking for her companions. She has forgotten they were hiding from her. Now the Witch just feels guilty for snapping at them. For the first time in days the Witch ventures into the hall, calling for her friends. "Guys come on down, I'm sorry. I shouldn't have shouted at you, come on let's go outside!".

Slowly the Frog pokes his head around the door and tentatively hops toward her. A few moments later the Pigeon flies down the stairs and settles on top of the banister. They stare at her reproachfully. "I'm sorry" the Witch repeats shamefully. She gets an accepting croak and coo in response. The Witch unlocks the back door and opens it with a flourish. The rain has stopped and the sun gleams, highlighting the drops of water glistening across the gutter. The Pigeon immediately swoops up into the trees fanning its feathers in the fresh air. The Frog delightedly leaps into a newly formed puddle and rolls around. The Witch looks on, feeling content for the first time since the date. She sighs and dials a number on her phone. The man answers. "Hello, it's me from the other day, I'm sorry about our date…"

True friends are the sunshine of life

◆ ◆ ◆

THE CIRCADIAN RHYTHM OF THE MOON

The moon is full tonight and the Witch must make her way to the gathering of her kind. Under moon light, she is not tired. Senses are sharpened and she feels the embrace of nature as she makes her way through the forest. As she moves intentionally along the path, her cloak flows from her shoulders like clouds running from her feet. An unexpected sound catches her attention. She stops dead in her tracks her ear tuned to the direction of the sound.

'No one could be foolish enough to follow me here' she thinks to herself. But no, there it is again – a soft whispering voice. With raised attention, her eyes scan the darkness for signs of movement. The whisper sound arrives again barely discernible to the sharpest of hearing. 'Take my hand Witch, I'll take you to a place no one knows' repeats the unseen whisper from the woods. The Witch wonders who would dare follow her into the sacred woods on this night when the power of the full moon will be the strongest.

The whispering voice continues. 'You gave away the love I gave you and so we end where we began'. The Witch drops the hood from her head to reveal her wild straw like hair, long to her shoulders. She brushes her hair away from her ear to listen closer. 'Let be seen' she calls out across the darkness, her squinting eyes focused to catch even the smallest of movement.

The only sound back is the rustling of the trees in the moon light as though taunting the young Witch as they dance to their own rhythm. The Witch peers to the darkness intently. Standing square, she glances over her shoulder towards her destination point and then up at the Moon nearing its high point. I can't miss the ceremony she thinks to herself before glancing again into the dark for a sign of the taunting voice.

Clasping her silver neck charm with one hand, she turns back to the path resolving to return to this place of whispers. Moving on she sees her fellow moon dancers have arrived and are preparing the circle. The moon light makes their de-cloaked skin glow silver contrasting against the green of the forest floor. As the Witch nears her destination, a sudden change in the path startles the Witch. She senses the presence of another close to her but can see no one. 'Is someone there?' she calls with an unexpected shake in her voice not customary for a Witch of powers. 'Only in fear, we end where we begin' is the response back to Witch. There is a very slow, deep pulse now reverberating through the floor of the forest that the Witch can feel through her feet. The low frequency pulse, slower than a heartbeat, causes the Witch's skin to prickle, and a sense of unknown fear. If you place your feet on the floor, you will feel it too.

A firm hand on the Witch's shoulder turns her quickly. A sister moon dancer standing before her places a hand over the Witch's mouth as though to prevent the Witch calling out and whispers softly.

'Someday, someone will look at you with a light in their eyes that you have never seen before. They'll look at you like you are everything. Wait for it then let them in'.

The Shining

'Would you like another coffee?' asks the man across the table over the centrally placed table candle. The Witch nods affirmation although not overly fond of strong coffee. The getting to know you date has gone well so far and no point in rocking the boat. 'So, are you worried that the coffee might keep you awake all night?' asks the Witch trying to keep the flow of conversation going. 'I think I might be immune to caffeine' says the man waving one hand in the air as though dismissing the waiter.

'I've never had a problem sleeping after drinking coffee' he continues. The Witch is eyeing her coffee date up and down. He's fairly pleasing on the eye, she thinks to herself and I guess I could get over the cappuccino colour suit that looks like it came from a charity shop in 1982. 'Nope, coffee has never had any affect on me' the man continues, proud that his immune system has found an antidote to the effects of caffeine. 'That's just amazing' exclaims the Witch sounding slightly sarcastic. 'So tell me more about what you do' she continues hoping to move him off the topic of coffee. 'Well, at the moment, I'm between opportunities and weighing up my options' continues the man as he sips on his fourth cup of coffee. 'And what do you do yourself?' he asks, 'I didn't see a job description on your SnatchdotCom dating profile'.

The Witch eyes him up across the table. Her pointed hat on the table and her broom standing by the doorway. Her cloak the darkest shade of black. 'Well, I would have thought that might be obvious' she cackles across the table at her new date. She rolls her fingers through the rising candle smoke showing off her long fingernails. The man is peering back at the Witch but has a confused look on his face. 'Well, I don't think you're a bus driver' he snorts, laughing loudly showing his back teeth to anyone who might be looking. 'But seriously, what do you do when you're not drinking coffee with strange men?' continues the inquisitor while the waiter refills his coffee cup for the fifth time.

The Witch is now also looking confused as she stares back at the man. 'You do remember that I arrived here on a broom?' says the Witch nodding her head at the same time. The man responds as though a light bulb has come on inside his head. 'Ahh…. Yes of course. The sweeping broom and the hooded cape, I should have known. You're a hairstylist?'

'Erm…. not exactly. I like to look at the moon at certain times, get excited about stars and dance with some close friends around a fire. Sometimes I like to be in the dark'.

The man looks across the table to the Witch, the whites of his eyes are starting to glow probably from caffeine overdose. 'Once you have been in the dark, you learn to appreciate everything that shines.'

Sometimes it hard to explain what you see in another person. It's the way they take you to a place no one else can.

Fairypainter

'I'm melting in this heat' complains the Witch to the Pigeon on her shoulder. The pair are out walking the village on a hot sunny day. The Pigeon of course doesn't respond to the Witch, as Pigeons' generally don't talk. In the centre of the village, there is a couple of craft stands, locals selling their efforts. The Witch is drawn to the stall of a young artist. 'Mmm…. this is interesting' thinks the Witch as she examines a picture of a fairy fantasy scene. The young artist approaches the Witch. 'Hello, can I help you with anything today' she squeaks. The Witch lifts her eyes from the painting to see a young girl almost as fairy like as her paintings. Her clothing style suggests bohemian fairy wearing a shirt with a print of a Pigeon that is familiar to the Witch.

'Do you know Pigeons?' inquires the Witch nodding towards the fairy painter's shirt. 'Ahh....not personally, responds the fairy painter. The Pigeon on the Witch's shoulder is flapping at the sight of the pigeon shirt. 'OMG, you have a Pigeon' squeaks the fairy painter as though just noticing the bird. The Witch strokes the Pigeon gently to calm the excitable bird. 'Can I touch your Pigeon?' asks the fairy painter reaching her arm forward without permission. The Witch drops her arm away submissively and the Pigeon appears to be enjoying this unexpected attention cooing like a contented bird as the fairy painter strokes its feathers.

The overhead sun is high, and beads of sweat are starting to run down the face of the Witch. 'You should remove your cloak' speaks the fairy painter – 'it is so warm today; you must be melting. I can loan you a t-shirt if you'd like?' The Witch concedes that it was probably not a good idea to wear the heavy black cape today and accepts the offer from the fairy painter.

The Witch extends her hand to accept willingly. She sets the Pigeon gently onto the painters table and lifts the heavy black cape over her head willingly exchanging for the light cotton shirt. 'It's a bit tight' she mutters looking down at her exposed mid riff. 'I think I might need a bigger size; this is like a boob tube on me' she exclaims trying to stretch the shirt longer to cover her naval.

Suddenly in silence, the Witch looks up quickly to see that she is no longer standing at the fairy painters stall, but alone in a grassy field. There is no one else around her and the hour has changed from day to night. She feels the dewy grass cold on her bare feet and a sense of loss befalls the Witch. Looking to the stars, the small size shirt is constraining and feels like a bandage instead of a shirt. Quickly she realizes that she has lost her powers and was duped by the fairy painter into handing over her magic. Now the Witch is standing alone in a field at night wearing a small white t-shirt with a pigeon logo and something about a frog not being a pigeon on the front.

Don't focus on what you don't have at the cost of ignoring what you do. Some people don't appreciate what they have until its gone.

◆ ◆ ◆

Longitude (by Isobelle)

"Watch it!" snaps the Witch. "OMG sorry" squeals a girl who has just tripped over the Witch. The Witch glares after her. She is the eighth person to trip over her since arriving at this forsaken field of noise. The Witch is uncomfortable amid the swirling crowds not of her own people.

Of course, it was the man's idea to go to a festival. She had stubbornly refused. "Festivals are not my scene" she had insisted, the man gazed at her with his mystifying eyes casting her under his spell. She had reluctantly agreed, on a promise, but now she was regretting that decision. They travelled for hours on buses surrounded by over excited "groupies" decked out in glitter and neon clothing. To be fair, the man did try to convince the Witch to wear "festival appropriate" attire but she refused in favour of her usual black get up and broom, perhaps slightly more in vogue at a Banshee gathering.

Her outfit was now attracting attention as many of the festival goers gawked at her. There is a sea of people moving in every direction, clamouring to see their favourite artists. The Witch can proudly say she doesn't know any. The Witch cannot wait to leave and return to the safety of her home as her heart pangs at the thought of the Frog and the Pigeon alone. Sniff.

"Are you alright?" the man inquires, concerned. "I'm fine" sighs the Witch, "just tired." "Are you sure?" the man looks doubtful. "Yeah, I just need some water" the Witch replies attempting to look like she's enjoying herself. "Ok I'll go grab some for you, stay right here, ok?" The Witch hates the sad sympathetic look on his face, the pity she knows he feels for her. Most of all she hates that she's ruining his day. Nevertheless, she nods and beams at him watching him dejectedly trudge through the crowds. The Witch contemplates leaving, almost certain the man will have a better time with her gone. She could just fly out of here on her broom, no bus rides or queues.

She begins to position her broom, when she hears a delighted squeal. She turns to see a young woman decked in sheer black dotted with stars, quite like the Witch's outfit. Glitter sparkles in pink crimped hair. "I absolutely *love* your outfit!" the girl exclaims, "Did you make it yourself? Unbelievable!" Her enthusiasm is contagious, and the Witch can't help feeling pleased. "Yes, I did" she informs her, with a hint of pride. "Same! I didn't think anyone would be wearing the same" she pauses. "Me and my buddies are heading over to the tent across the bridge, my favourite artist is playing and is so chilled, nothing like this head banging rubbish" she rolls her eyes. The Witch feels a glimmer of hope. "Yeah that sounds amazing, I'll head over soon I'm waiting for someone". The girl waves and hurries after her friends. The Witch feels better, much better. She can't wait for the man to get back, for them to go to the tent and for them to start enjoying themselves. The Witch smiles closing her eyes and leaving the music wash over her.

Choosing to see the good, even when it's hard will bring you where you want to be.

Sacred Geometry

'Let's deal the cards' cries out the Witch. The Pigeon perched on the table to her right side and the Frog to her left, hold council for their master. The Witch deals a card from East to West, and North to South, as nagging voices of memories whisper in her mind, some distant and some near.

'Deal me Witch' she hears a voice in her mind. Without lifting her eyes, the Witch selects a card from the deck and places it on the table in front of her. With a quick flick of her wrist she turns the card on the table and peers to the image expectantly, looking to read the pattern in the card and to see what she hopes to see. 'Mmm... I see a man calling' muses the Witch aloud as she interprets the sacred geometry of the tarot. The Pigeon flaps nervously to distract the Witch from hopeful thinking. She turns her eyes to the Pigeon.

Extending her soft hand towards the bird to comfort the creature, she stokes the blue / grey feathers. The bird continues to flap but starts to calm with each stroke. 'Don't worry so much' continues the Witch, 'regrets are past and cannot be changed'. The Pigeon coo's as though understanding.

The Witch draws the next card and places it face up in front of her. 'Ahh... I see vulnerability, the cost of striving to achieve.' The Frog croaks as though to signal that he is present and resents the excessive attention paid to the old Pigeon. The Witch senses the frog's neediness and repositions the bowl of water closer to the creature as a gesture of comfort. She also senses her stolen powers returned and feels her deep connection to this moment. Her breath has become shallow as she feels her heart beating steady. If you listen carefully now, you will hear it too.

Slowly, the walls of the room seem to fade away and she feels a light summer breeze against her face. Opening her eyes in sunlight, she hears the muffled voices of her brother McNnif and the Viking woman Togram. In this dream state, she sees past relationships now gone and thoughts flood her mind of what if, and if only and why. She feels a heavy heart as these thoughts pass through like a flock of pigeons startled to flight in her mind. Waving her hand in the air, as though to clear the imaginary birds, the Witch feels her mind settle back to the present, back to her breath, back to her heartbeat.

As the Witch's eyes slowly open back to the kitchen table the Pigeon is strutting up and down on the table breathing heavily like a bird after a hard-spinning class. The Witch opens the palm of her hand and the Pigeon willingly accepts. Standing to her feet, she gently carries the Pigeon to the open window and releases the bird to the sky.

Sometimes, we keep past regrets and memories to the front of our mind. Every now and then, let the past out of your mind, let them fly while you enjoy the present. Past experience is the compass to the future not the path.

We are frogsnotpigeons. A story brand from Ireland.

SINGLE USE PLASTIC

Waiting her turn, the Witch is uncomfortable in public settings. She is attending at the job centre after receiving an official letter to review her current 'employment status'. Eventually, her number is called, and she approaches the vacant seat at the designated hatch. Behind the counter, an unhappy looking soul looks the Witch straight as though eyeing up the last chocolate square. 'Would you mind removing the hat please?' starts the grump in a dismissive tone. The Witch is already uncomfortable but concedes to the request. 'Your name and date of birth' barks the grump through teeth and the plastic screen, both yellowed with age.

The Witch is uneasy and pushes the appointment letter through the small opening towards the stern looking grump. Without any acknowledgement, the grump accepts the letter and turns to the PC to confirm details.
Whilst the grump is busy pushing buttons, the Witch's attention is drawn to the raised voice at the adjoining hatch where there is a one-way animated discussion in progress about some perceived injustice and entitlement. From where the Witch is sitting, it looks like the person is having an argument with themselves as there is no audible response from the other side of the plastic screen.

'What is your occupation?' asks the grump muffled behind the screen. The Witch turns back to the official behind the plastic.

'I'm a practicing Witch' she answers in a soft tone trying not to become part of the public display for others, unlike the person next to her. 'I can't lip read' calls the official back louder as though to ensure those to follow can hear. The Witch leans closer and repeats 'I'm a Witch' in a stronger tone.

The grump on the other side looks frozen staring back at the Witch as though in a trance. 'Did you get that?' asks the Witch back into the screen. The grump squints it's eyes and snaps back loudly 'Don't be so defensive crone, I'm just doing my job'. The Witch is taken aback by the tone but also not used to communication through a plastic screen. 'I'm not defensive' retorts the Witch, 'and I'm not a crone either'.

'Look love, unlike you, I don't have a crystal ball, and this is the jobs centre not Hogwarts' responds the grump. 'I was born into the craft' responds the Witch shifting about uncomfortably on the plastic seat. The grump shakes its head turning back to the keyboard, mutters, and finger types 'craft worker'.

The Witch looks about her and realizes that she is now the focus of attention for the other souls waiting. Looking down at her own hand, she notices her painted nails, long and sharp. Placing her hand onto the plastic screen she scratches into the plastic with her nails.

The grump behind the plastic glares back. The Witch puts on her hat and leans into the plastic screen and in a loud voice. 'No title can define who you are'. With a swish of her cape turns to leave. On the plastic is the words etched;

Be someone who makes you happy.

Echos

A roll of thunder has awoken the Witch. It's unusual weather at this time of year, thinks the Witch as she wraps her cape to her shoulders to venture down to the kitchen. A flash of lightning lights up the narrow stairway followed by thunder. The Witch stumbles into her kitchen where she finds the Pigeon sleeping, its head under its wing breathing heavily. Another flash of lightning lights the kitchen. 'This is unusual weather' speaks the Witch to herself, 'someone has caused upset to the goddess'. As the thunder rolls, she sees the Frog under the table and gently lifts the creature into the sink for safety. 'You're safer in the sink' she speaks softly to the creature, 'if your stepped on by the horse foot Viking woman, it will not be pretty'.

The next flash of lightning lights up the garden through the window. The Witch catches glimpse of unexpected shapes outside. 'Now, what was that?' she asks herself out loud. As she cautiously opens the back door she peers into the darkness and can briefly make out hooded shapes standing motionless in the garden. Clouds are moving fast across the sky that cast shadows to the ground like dancing elves.

Taking her staff from inside the back door she steps into the garden. From this position she can make out hooded figures standing in a closed circle made by joining hands. As she steps towards the group, the circle opens partly, and she notices a man standing in the centre of the circle beckoning her forward. The storm passes over with lightning flashes in the distance. Summer rain is pouring down and with wind creates its own sound above all others as it beats the summer dry leaves and branches of the trees overhead.

'Who are you?' shouts the Witch as she nears the circle entrance made for her. 'What brings you here?' she continues not sure to be heard over the wind and rain. At the edge of the cloaked circle, she pauses knowing that the next step will enable the circle to close behind her. The man at the centre beckons her forward. She feels the circle of hands close behind her. 'East then South, then West then North' chants the cloaked circle out over the summer storm. The Witch feels the energy surround her. She is not afraid. As the noise of storm and voices fades into the background the Witch feels a strength embrace her, not menacing but comforting, protecting. Against her skin the Witch is aware of the breath of another on her skin. Like oak or burnt wood, it's a scent her memory is familiar with. She feels sadness in the echo of a heartbeat from a time past.

The moment is suddenly disturbed by an unexpected sound of a bird. 'Coo... Coo. The sound repeats with more urgency, Coo.... COO.

Suddenly, the vision is released, and a voice breaks the darkness 'Will you let that flipping Pigeon out' calls the angry voice. The Witch glares back with contempt and a deep sense of loss.

In dreams, we see places and events as our mind wants them to be. Dreams are only constrained by the self-imposed reality we choose for ourselves.

The Frog and the Girl

Ever since he was a tadpole, the frog watched people visit the edge of the water. The same girl would visit every morning to watch the sun rising, acknowledge the earth and the water spirits and sit in deep thought for a time before leaving to go about her day. Usually, the girl stood carefree, reaching her arms to the sky and then kneeling to the ground before taking a seated place next to the water edge. Sometimes, she left small treats for the Frog and others that shared the water's edge. The Frog didn't know this girl but imagined her at school or college doing exams and had grown to appreciate the daily visitor.

One morning, the girl appeared as usual, but this time looked unhappy and instead of taking her usual seat on the ground, stood firm as though expecting the worst. The Frog noticed the girl shake her head at the sky and depart again. The Frog hoped that the girl would return the next sunrise in happier spirit. However, the following morning the girl did not appear and with the passing of each day the Frog began to give up hope for the girl appearing at the water side again. After nearly a full moon phase, the Frog had sadly given up hope of seeing the girl again. Then one August summer morning, the Frog surfaced in the pond to see the young girl sitting on the bank of the water's edge. Her hair had grown longer but it was her. The Frog swam to the water's edge excited and jumped out on to the bank. The Frog croaked but the girl's sadness did not break. The Frog remembered that humans do not understand language of others and recalled how he communicated with the Witch through heart speak. The Frog approached the young girl and with great courage stretched his webbed feet forward to touch the skin of the young girl. 'Hello' he croaked as loud as he could. The girls stare broke and she peered down at the Frog. 'Did you just speak?' she said in a quivering voice. The Frog beamed with a smile acknowledging contact. The Frog watched in amazement as water started to fall from the young girl's face. 'Your raining!' exclaimed the Frog. The girl shook her head. 'They are tears. But, how can it be that I am talking with a Frog?'

'Perhaps your rain has unblocked your heart so that you can hear me' said the Frog with a smile. The girl nodded and explained that she has visited the pond for many months giving thanks for everything and yet was still worried for what the future holds. 'Others have great expectations of me, and I am angry with myself that I may fail those expectations' she cried. The Frog thought for a moment about how the Witch had told him that anger hides real emotions blinding the heart with hate. 'What is underneath your anger?' asks the Frog.

The girl thought for a second. 'I'm afraid that I may not be good enough' she answered.

Frog patted the girls arm with his webbed feet to offer comfort. 'Fear traps us so that we can't move. It's like being stuck in a hole and the more we let it, the more it will close around us.' said the

Frog.

The girl looked down at the Frog and a single drop of eye rain fell onto his head. 'What should I do?' asked the girl.

'Move!' said the Frog. It's easy to become trapped in what might happen. Sometimes the only way to not be trapped is to decide not to be.

The Interview

Like many other groups, to become a member, a candidate is interviewed by the Witch before accepted for initiation. It's a bit like a job interview in some ways but without the complication of what to wear.

The Witch is sitting opposite a candidate that has expressed interest in joining the frogsnotpigeons coven. Perched beside the Witch at the table is her companion, the Pigeon. From across the table, the Witch and the candidate look each other up and down momentarily. Perhaps not surprising, realizing they are both dressed in similar attire.

The pair sit for a moment in an awkward silence that chills the room.

'So, what's your interest in frogsnotpigeons?' asks the Witch. The candidate places both elbows on the table intertwining her two hands under her chin as though to prevent her mouth opening.

'Mmm... I thought I could help reduce the average age of the group' mutters the candidate.

'Do you have experience of using Social Media platforms like FrogSnap, Chanting or Circle Casting?' asks the Witch stroking the Pigeon gently.

The interviewee rubs her hands together as though exfoliating after a recent pond moisturising session. She turns her head sideways and looks down to her feet where a black cat is curled around her ankle.

'Ah, come up here Kitty' she calls to the cat.

The cat jumps to the table and before it has settled the candidate runs her presumably super soft hand down its arching back. The cat purrs contentment and sits on its hind quarters while the Pigeon flaps its wings nervously at the sight of the cat before settling again under the calmness of the Witch's gentle stroke.

'You have a black cat?' speaks the Witch. 'Well, it's not a racehorse' retorts the candidate snorting loudly through her nose. The Witch is getting unsettled and, in her mind, has already decided that this candidate is not a good fit for the coven. 'Perhaps we will leave it for the moment and will come back to you on the next stage' says the Witch as she pushes her chair back to get to her feet. 'We don't really do the black cat thing' continues the Witch waving one hand in the air, slightly dismissively. 'We are more of the water and air creatures – like the frog and pigeon' she finishes.

The candidate begins a recital. 'By all the power of three times three, this spell bound around shall be.' Recognizing the chant, the Witch reaches to her pocket and removes her hazel wand to prevent the spell from casting. In a flash, the small room is filled with a fog and a commotion that is heard but not seen. As the fog clears, the candidate has gathered the cat in her arms and hurriedly leaves. The Witch gladly opens the exit door only to notice the trailing of blue feathers on the floor behind the candidate leaving and the smile on the face of the cat as though just finished its dinner.

Sometimes we lose sight of what's important instead focusing on issues and events that are transient and don't last. Look around you and make sure that you don't lose sight of what's important while focusing on the meaningless chatter, that is ultimately, only background noise. Also, don't bring a cat to an interview.

The Listening Tree

At the center of the forest, or woodlands there is a tree that stands proud above others. The Sun shines its warming light between the leaves and the rain spirits sometimes rest upon them before falling to the ground. This is the Listening Tree with deep roots that reach down into the Earth and with tall branches that reach to the sky. For as long as the Witch can remember, people have visited the Listening Tree to tell of heavy hearts and share sad stories. Some place a hand on the tree bark and silently share their burden with the great tree. Others sit at the base of the tree with their backs touching the trunk and yet others want to hug the tree as though trying to pick up the great tree from the ground. The latter are called tree huggers, but all leave less burdened, standing taller and with a hint of renewed hope in their eyes.

The Witch thinks to herself about what stories the tree must have heard and yet it stands tall and proud fixed to the earth and reaching towards the sky. Never sharing secrets only ever listening, providing support for all who need it.

As the Witch places her hands to the bark of the tree, she closes her eyes and feels her own heartbeat. Somewhere, in the distance of her imagination, she hears the wind chimes of worry jangling. If you listen closely now, you might hear it too.

As her breathing becomes shallow, she feels the strength of the great tree embrace her like a slow dance on a night club floor with someone familiar. The Witch feels herself lighten as future worries fade to the distance with only the sparks from an inner battle dancing around in her mind. She feels a strong hand in the middle of her back, as the 'dancer' pulls the Witch closer, then a little closer, so that she can feel the strong presence surround her that makes her fears come to the front of her mind. A whisper speaks to her ear softly. 'You're frightened because I answered'. For a second, the Witch is lost in the moment and not sure of the meaning of the voice.

As the slow dance comes to an end, she realizes that the inner battle in her mind is fear of an event in the future that has not happened. Resolving in that moment to release the fear, to stop calling out to an event that has not happened, to live in the present, she feels a deep sense of relief.

When people feel they can speak to nobody else, when the secrets are too great or the sorrow too deep, the Listening Tree is always ready to hear. It stands ready to absorb sadness, anger, frustration, fear and every other emotion. However, when you find your tree, remember to share happiness too; allow it to take your problems and worries but remember to share joy and laughter also. If the tree is listening, it seems only right to share lightness to balance the shadows of our hearts.

If you call loud enough to problems that have not yet happened, someday, they might answer you.

SPELL CASTING
DISTRACTION

The Witch's cauldron is brewing, as she continues a gentle stir adding the prescribed ingredients to the pot. The Pigeon is near, bobbing to a rhythm as though listening to music in its head. The Frog is splayed out in the saucer of water, like some green nubile sunbathing in a private pool. Both make sure to keep out of the way in case added to the ingredients by mistake. The Witch begins her recital to magic the potion and give it power. 'Hail, guardians of the watchtowers of the South, powers of fire, send forth your flame, we invoke you now'. The Witch throws her arms to the sky, expectant. A steam rises from the cauldron and fills the air creating its own strange aura.

Behind her, the silence of the casting is broken by a vibration sound that persists. The Witch ignores the worldly distraction as she focuses on the moment waiting to hear from her master on the other side. The sound stops, and the Witch continues the chant. 'Hail guardians of the watchtowers of the West, powers of water. We invoke you and call you'. As a silence falls on the scene, the Witch feels the presence of the goddess and knows that she is near. Suddenly, the persistent vibration starts again. The Witch tries to ignore, but the persistence of the sound breaks the trance and the Witch drops her arms to her side and grabs the mobile phone from nearby. 'What!' she screams down the phone. There is a slight pause as though the caller is surprised that there is an answer. 'Hi, my name is Daphne from customer care calling you about your mobile phone service. How are you?' The Witch takes a deep breath and calmly tells the caller 'I'm busy casting a spell, can you call another time thank you'. The caller hesitates, but only for a moment and then continues.

'Ah that's great, can you confirm your name and mobile number for me please for data protection?' The Witch shakes her head to herself and recites back a name and number to the caller hoping that this will end the conversation. 'And do you have a landline number please?' The Witch presses the red button on her phone and disconnects the call.

Turning back to the cauldron and the gathered members, 'right, where was I?'. As the Witch retakes her position, a glow has formed a circle around them. The Pigeon is flapping, a sure sign of presence. The Witch picks up a small stick and starts to beat out a strong pounding rhythm, 'Seed Sower, grain reborn, Horned One, Come!'. Other voices join the Witch. Hands clap out the rhythm on bare thighs; feet stamp the floor. There is one great shout 'Lo! Evohe'.

Then a sudden silence as the gathered frogsnotpigeons wait for their response.

Deringg.... Deringg....Deringg..... breaks the trance. The phone vibrates on the table in a persistence that calls out 'urgent, urgent'.

The Witch feels eyes on her, and the moment is broken. She turns quickly and places the phone to her ear. A soft-spoken voice from the other side. 'Hi, its Daphne again from customer care, can I just ask you to confirm your broadband speed please?'.

Life is full of distractions. Sometimes we loose focus on what's important because someone else is ringing their bell for us to answer.

Closer to You

The Witch looks down at the Pigeon, eyes wide and brow furrowed. 'What are you nattering on about bird?' she calls in a dismissive tone. The Pigeon steps from one foot to the other like on hot coals. 'If you just let me take your hand' coo's the bird. The Witch shakes her head slowly and purses her lips tight. 'Bird, I know you think you know me, but you don't' she speaks dismissively to the Pigeon.

The Pigeon flaps its wings annoyed. Still, stomping from one foot to the other, 'why can't you take me seriously?' 'Calm yourself bird, you'll do yourself injury' speaks the Witch as she softly strokes the feathers of the bird. 'What is it that has you agitated?' she continues. 'I want you to see me as more than just a flipping Pigeon' coo's the bird.

The Witch tilts her head looking down on the small creature. 'Perhaps you just need to get out a bit more' speaks the Witch as she turns her head away. 'Do you mean like; I should take the bus into town or something?' snaps the Pigeon in a sarcastic tone. 'You have more time for that lazy green frog that spends its day in a bowl of slime, blinking. I mean all the Frog seems to do is blink all day, what kind of attraction is that? At least I clean and prune regularly!' blurts the Pigeon.

The Witch turns herself back to the bird, 'Pigeon, we are not meant to be, you are of a different kind than me. Our personalities don't match'. The Pigeon flaps wildly and creates a sound with its wings that becomes rhythmic like a pounding. Suddenly, the bird takes to flight and goes out the open window leaving behind only small white feathers. The Witch watches the bird take to the sky and thinks if there was something that she should not have said.

Later that afternoon, there is a heavy knock to the back door. The Witch gets to her feet and quickly walks to the door. Opening, she is confronted by a tall stranger in a long cloak and brimmed hat that partially hides his face. 'Yes – what do you want?' asks the Witch holding the back door open with one hand but ready to slam it shut again at an instant. As the man lifts his head, the Witch notices the deep brown piercing eyes of the stranger. 'Are you still too scared to let me in?' speaks the man in a deep tone.

'Do you know me?' responds the Witch feeling her fingers twitch on the door ready to release should the need be. The tall stranger steps closer to the Witch and to her own surprise, she lets him. He reaches forward and take's her hand in his. Strangely, the Witch feels a magic about this man and a sense of familiarity as though knowing him a long time that sets aside her defences. 'This feeling is real; I know that for sure' speaks the man to the Witch's ear. In that moment, the Witch looks down to the ground and notices the small flurry of white downy feathers not dissimilar to those of a small bird....

Sometimes, what we search for is closer than we think.

The Spiral Dance

'Take my hand, let me take you to a place that no one knows'. The Witch looks up into the dark eyes staring back at her. Initially, she is hesitant. Experience tells her that she has been here before and is tired from disappointment. Her sadness betrayed by her face as she wipes away a tear, but only small tear, rolling from her face. The Witch feels strong arms embrace her, wrapping a cloak or darkness around her and drawing her in. She knows this feeling from before and sets aside hesitation to welcome Pan's return. The darkness has closed around them and the Witch feels her feet lift from the ground. She is no longer who she was.

The Witch is sky bound, carried along in a hooded cloak, she feels the rush of autumn wind and hears the roll of thunder in the distance. She recognizes the seasonal dance between the departure of summer and the arrival of autumn. The spiral dance continues as the pair cross the divide into the other world. The

Witch senses that they have arrived at another place as she feels the cloaked embrace finally release her. She opens her eyes to the sound of crashing waves on a beach front with the cloud dimmed light from the Moon Goddess watching down on the pair. The salt air hangs heavy on the breath as the flickering stars tease those watching dancing in and out among the fast-moving clouds.

'Why have you vanished me to this place?' calls the Witch over the crashing of the sea. 'Your mistaken' speaks Pan, 'you are as visible to me now as you have always been'. The Witch pulls her cloak closer to protect against the autumn chill as she looks about her, scanning the horizon as though doubting herself. 'I don't understand, I'm pretty sure we are standing on a beach in the moonlight' she calls back as she feels the wet sand beneath her feet. She feels a gentle touch on her arm and his warm breath to her face as he touches lips to her cheek. The Witch feels a shiver. This time, it is not from the cold.

'Twice before, you have turned your back on me' speaks the Witch. 'You are mistaken again' responds Pan, 'for I have never turned from you'. The Witch reaches for the hood covering the dark watcher's face that she might see clear the face of who has brought her to this place. In the moment, the noise from the sea crashing fades so that it is no longer heard. It is silent and calm. Stepping up on her toes, the Witch whispers to the man's ear, 'you touched my cheek and vanished me to this place – tell me the purpose we are here?'

The dark watcher with tangled brow, places a finger to his lips to hear no more of promises that we will never keep. Nor of the secret dream that slips away as we rise from sleep.

Life only comes around once. Do whatever makes you happy and be with whoever makes you smile. Don't waste your time with people who want to find fault with everything and everyone.

Hurtful Words

"Oh no, what does *SHE* want now" cries out the Witch on noticing the approach of the Viking woman, Togram, coming up the drive way. As the burly woman approach's the front door like a ram raid, the Witch swings it open. The Witch's facial expression changes as she greets the Viking with a broken tooth smile. "What a surprise" she calls out, "so nice to see you, is it a week already?" The two women share an awkward embrace. "Still washing your hair in horse urine?" asks Togram, "the shine is nice but not sure about the 'ode de toilet'". The Witch doesn't respond to the criticism and instead ushers her unwanted guest through to the Kitchen. "So, what do I owe the pleasure of your visit Togram?" asks the Witch.

"I hear that you have a new man called Fan or something" blurts Togram, as blunt as a hammer as usual. The Witch seats herself at the Kitchen table, pre-empting the inquisition about to follow. "Well, his name is Pan and, yes we've had a date, but its early days yet". Togram hesitates a second but decides to press on with the inquisition; "Is this another one from that Smash.com?" she presses on, "you know that on-line dating doesn't end well for you when you don't even put up your real picture".

The Witch blushes slightly, as only some do. Flicking her wild hair from her face, she looks up to see the Viking woman smirk. The Witch feels the Viking woman circling her as though a bird of prey ready to strike. She cups her hands nervously in front of her like in prayer and lifts her eyes slightly to see her own faded reflection in the mirror. "Witch, you need to stay with your own, and stop this finding happiness nonsense" cuts Togram's voice like a sharp blade through warm chocolate sponge.

The back window suddenly swings open and there is a loud noise of flapping wings – the Kitchen is filled with Pigeons coo'ing and circling those present like a demented flock of birds looking for sanctuary from a hunting cat in a confined space. The Witch stands to her feet feeling the power of the Pigeons call her – 'he is here, he is here, – the Comforter, the Consoler, Hearts Ease, and Sorrow's end in the Dance of Shadows'. Togram is gone into hysterics as the Pigeons fly wildly around her head grazing with sharp beaks. She makes a line towards the open door, waving her arms above her head wildly to fend off the flying rats, screaming profanity, she departs the same way she arrived.

The Witch stands centre in the swirl of birds as they circle her. She doesn't feel afraid. The effect is hypnotic as she extends her arms showing her white palms as though offering a landing perch to the circling Pigeons. Instead she feels another hand in hers. A strong hand that holds tight, it squeezes but doesn't hurt, instead offers comfort. 'We are in sight of the shore, see the light on the waves, a shroud, a track to follow. Step into the surf, step ashore. Cast of your bonds and be free!' she hears over the call of the birds.

A smile crosses the Witch's face and she breaths deep. She realizes hurtful words from others have no meaning unless you give them meaning. Not everyone deserves to know the real you.

MEETING THE
OTHER CROWD

Relationships, as they go, generally requires meeting the others as though a seal of approval is required. The Witch is no different. Standing at the doorway, she waits nervously. From the outside, it looks dark and foreboding, not a welcoming place. 'So here you are' calls a voice from inside. 'Enter freely into the house of Pan, for here there is no binding. Cast off the veils Witch, that cloud your sight'. Oh Oh… the Witch thinks, this doesn't sound good. Lifting her hands slowly she drops her hood to let her wild hair escape and steps inside.

She waits for someone familiar to validate her presence in this unfamiliar place. She doesn't wait long as she feels a hand take hers and turns to see Pan leading her deeper into the house. He gently places his lips to hers and she feels him breathe a smoky breath into her lungs. 'Come meet the others' he speaks softly. By the light of a fire, she sees an Old Crone, barely distinguishable in the darkness lit only by the flickers from the fire burning in the fireplace.

Pan sweeps his hand away from the Witch towards the Old Crone as though beckoning her to step closer. The Old Crone lifts her eyes slowly and raises her withered hand towards the Witch. Without hesitating, the Witch reaches forward and takes the Old

Crones invite. As their hands touch, the Witch feels the loneliness of the Old Crone race up her arm to her body. 'You are welcome here Witch of the coven frogsnotpigeons' speaks the Crone. 'We won't hold it against you where you're from'. The Witch nods her head and leans forward; 'So nice to meet you' she speaks softly back to the Old Crone, 'I have heard much about you'. The Old Crone nods understanding but disbelieving. 'So, how did you meet him?' asks the Old Crone. 'Well, we have known each other for a time, although I didn't recognise him' answers the Witch now starting to relax. 'Ah yes, Pan has many masks' cackles the Old Crone, laughingly, a private joke not appreciated by the Witch.

Looking beyond the flickering fire light the Witch can see only darkness surround them. 'Your home is nice' speaks the Witch hoping to move the conversation on. 'Where did you get your curtains, the double lining is very effective' she continues. The Crone rocks back and forth from her seat not taking the new conversation direction. 'Sit beside me here on the floor, that I can see you better. The Witch obediently takes a place on the floor beside the Old Crone. 'We are nearing Samhain time, known in your world as Halloween' croaks the Old Crone – 'you will join us tonight in the harvest circle'. 'Oh, please don't go to any trouble for me, I was only dropping in to say hello' speaks the Witch nervously. The Old Crone ignores the young Witch and leans forward to place a woven straw chord over the Witches head around her neck. 'Behold the circle of rebirth and the cord of life. In this place, your light will never fade'. The Crone leans into the Witch and whispers softly; 'The tragedy of life is not death but what we let die inside of us'.

Remember, that life is not measured by the number of breaths we take but by the moments that take our breath away.

Natural Frequency

'What's the matter with you Frog?' asked the Witch reaching down towards the Frog dropping some dead flies to the water's edge. 'Not hungry,' the Frog replied in a croaky voice. 'I can feel your mood' said the Witch, 'you seem not yourself lately'. The Frog stretched back his knobbly legs but said nothing. The Witch waited. She knew she had not paid much attention to the Frog in some time busy with her own life. She reached her index finger down to the Frog and gave him a gentle nudge. 'The water nymphs tell me you might be off colour or a bit depressed,' the Witch prodded, 'and if *they* notice a bad mood, it must be serious. You know how they keep themselves busy and don't notice anything else going on around them'. The Frog rested his chin onto his front leg but still said nothing. 'Come on Frog' said the Witch, 'this is not like you. Nobody expects a Frog to be the life and soul of the party, but a few croaks every now and then would be nice.'

'I just don't feel like doing much' croaked the Frog softly. 'I woke up feeling this way and I don't know why.' The Witch stroked her chin wondering for a moment. 'Has something been bothering you?' she asks.

The Frog shook its head. 'I know your trying to help, Witch, but I fear I might be beyond comfort today,' He sniffed loudly, and a single drop of slime ran down his cheek. The Witch thought for a moment and then gently reached down to cup the frog in her two hands and lifted the Frog from the slimy pond. 'What are you doing?' croaked the Frog glumly. 'I feel your sadness,' she said gently. 'You may be hiding under your blanket of slime, but we are all connected, and your sadness sends ripples out to others around you. I am worried about you'. The Frog blinked sadly, and another droplet ran down his cheek. 'I don't want to feel like this,' he croaked, 'but I don't know how to shake it off'.

The Witch walked out into the nearby forest and placed the small Frog onto a rock so that it could see its surrounding. A small bird flew down and landed on the ground in front of the Frog. 'When I'm feeling down, I flap my wings and it always makes me feel good' whistled the bird lifting itself into the air again. 'We like to dig holes everywhere' said a pair of young rabbits, diving back into a mound of clay. The Frog suddenly felt something land close by him and looked up just in time to avoid another hitting him. 'We like to throw acorns' giggled the squirrels from the tree branches above. 'You little tree rats!' shouts the Frog back, laughing as he jumped up and down on his rock to avoid the missiles. 'How are you feeling now?' asks the Witch gently. 'Are you any happier?'

The Frog smiled: 'as a matter of fact, I feel much better, thank you'.

'You're welcome,' said the Witch. 'We don't always know why we feel sad, but there is always a way to find your smile. Sometimes, you just need to dance around for a while and your smile will find you'.

The Circumplex Model of Emotion

As the Witch tossed a couple of beach stones, enjoying the solitude and the sound of the sea, she notices the approaching figure of a familiar walk. 'No, it can't be!' exclaims the Witch out loud to herself. Focusing her eyes on the approaching person, the Witch recognizes the walk of the Viking Woman Togram coming towards her along the beach. 'She must have the scent of a blood hound to find me here' thinks the Witch as she quickly jumps to her feet, dusting sand off, wondering if she can escape before Togram gets closer. Almost at the same time, Togram raises her arm in a lumbering wave as though warning a large ship of danger close by. 'She sees me', thinks the Witch as she feebly acknowledges Togram's signal.

As the Viking Woman nears, barefoot, carrying her shoes in one hand, like a bedraggled debutant who missed her bus home, a smile broadens across her face. 'Ah, Witch, I thought it was you when I saw your straw hair blowing' 'Yes, yes.... so nice to see you' stutters the Witch through a forced smile. 'Are you here by yourself?' continues Togram making an exaggerated scan around the Witch as though looking for someone hiding behind her. The Witch wonders why some people ask questions about the obvious. 'Its just me' she responds coyly through another forced grin. 'Ah that's a shame' responds Togram. The Witch nods her head slowly, pursing her lips tightly as though to prevent someone force feeding her lemons.

Togram links the arm of the Witch and turns her to take a walk along the beach. 'So, tell me, what's the news on the new man?' asks Togram leaning closer into the Witch. 'Not much to tell' responds the Witch in a matter of fact tone. 'Really, your eyes look so much brighter in last few weeks, the make-up suits you', exclaims Togram in a questioning tone. The Witch decides to change the topic. 'What's your news, what brings you out here to the beach'? asks the Witch. Togram, nods her head and seems to hesitate before responding. 'I'm listening to the Doubting Fairy a lot lately, who keeps telling me I'm not good enough. Can't seem to shake him from my dreams lately' croaks Togram.

The Witch, surprised, glances across at Togram beside her and notices her eyes are heavy and filled with sadness. 'I told you before Togram, that defeating the Doubting Fairy once can make him stronger and only the bravest of hearts may succeed in their quest. In order to beat the Doubting Fairy once and for all, you must question every fear that rise's inside you. You will see that thoughts are just thoughts and can be dismissed by choice. You will also find that the negative self-beliefs that you thought true are false all along. Each of us is challenged with the confusion between excitement and fear but that you have the absolute ability to choose either emotion.'

Togram looked intently at the Witch. Eventually, a broad smile breaks out across her face as an understanding dawns inside her mind.

Sometimes, we just need to slow down and take small steps for thoughts are not truths. What are you thinking?

Witches Spinning.

With sustained effort, heart rates rise, the shortage of breath induces *mind drift* so that thoughts and dreams become mixed with reality.

The Witches gathered push open this door gladly, freely giving up to inner thoughts that releases them from the constraints of life. After a short time, our Witch lets her mind drift to a different place born of experience and memory. In the moment, she sees herself standing deep in the forest with light autumnal rain falling. The wind lifts the fallen leaves around her so that they look to be dancing to unheard music. The Witch raises her arms and lifts her face to look skyward through the tops of the tall trees. Breathing deeply, her bare feet firmly connected to mother earth as her cloak flaps wildly in the wind. She feels the power of life all around her.

The noise of the wind through the naked trees is loud as the trees appear to protest the weather by waving limbs wildly that looks like floss dancing. A little way ahead, the Witch notices movement in the undergrowth. Slowly, the Witch steps forward to approach where a tree has shed branches to the wind some hours earlier. Crouching to the ground the Witch peers closer between the leaves and the fallen branches and sees a pair of dark beady eyes staring back. Framed by the blackness of the wet leaves, the blinking eyes belong to a Wood Pigeon whose nest has fallen with the branches trapping the bird. Gently, the Witch reaches forward to clear some of the smaller branches and leaves from the terrified birds face. The Pigeon blinks wildly and lets out a shallow

Coo. The Witch realizes that this creature has not much more to give. Catching the Pigeons gaze, the Witch gets a strange feeling in her heart, an emotion that she has not felt in a long while. As the Witch's heart opens, she feels the energy of the forest surround her like a golden light in the misty rain. The Witch wills the energy to her and lifts the branches away releasing the trapped creature to fly away effortlessly into the trees.

The Witch feels her breath caught in her chest; long lost emotions begin to rise inside her. Wiping a tear mixed with rain from her face, the Witch stands and pushes her long hair from her face to over her shoulders.

She feels her breathing start to slow and the outline forms of her frogsnotpigeons sisters come back into focus. Bright colours of different clothing mixed with the deliberate movement of exercise make it appear as a sequenced dance routine visible through a haze of sweat evaporating from heated bodies.

As one of the others approaches the Witch. The Witch notices the stranger's beady eyes that look strangely familiar blinking rapidly from the exertion. 'Thank you, Witch, perhaps I'll see you at the next spinning class'.

The most attractive thing about someone is not how they look but how they choose to help others in need.

ARADIA GATHERS

The hooded of frogsnotpigeons are gathered to form a circle around the young Witch. Standing alone at the centre, she feels the power as they chant to the night sky. The Witch drops her caped hood to her shoulders and looks to the dark sky with the full moon glimpsing down through teasing breaks in the clouded sky. Casting her arms towards the sky she calls – 'Goddess of the Moon, we invite your presence'. The gathered continue the rhythmic chant that is almost hypnotic, holding each other's hands to form a chain of hooded cloaks around the Witch. The chant echoes across the night sky – 'Aradia, Aradia, Aradia…. 'It is the time of Halloween. Listen carefully and you will hear them.

After a short time, the Goddess of the Moon parts the clouds and looks down on those gathered. All are thankful for the light of the moon and the break in the clouds that is a welcome relief from the rain of recent days. They sense the goddess is with them looking down on her daughter standing in the circle centre in wait. 'The Witch raises her arms to the moon and cries out over the chanting coven. 'From you I received the breath of life, and unto you I give over my breath…'.

A silence follows as the chanting ebbs away. The presence of the Moon Goddess is felt in the appearance of a tall woman in a silver dress with stars sparkled across her cheek bones and through into her black hair as though her hair is the night sky. At the circle centre, both proud Witches acknowledge each other in silence.

'Before you were born, I had a vision of Arcadia in a dream,' whispers the Moon Goddess softly. 'She was the priestess who led us here to this place to begin our lives in harmony with nature, the moon and the stars. In fact, your name was given to you by Arcadia.' The Moon Goddess makes a gesture towards the fire ash and with invisible hand scrolls the word 'Arcadia' appears in the blackened ground. With a second gesture, the letter C is erased from the word to leave the name of Aradia, 'Know that many will tremble at your knowledge and woe unto any man that tries to still your hand of magic. You must be careful of this new man called Pan. He is known with many names and wears many masks – what you see is but one.' The Witch nods her head in understanding 'it is early days yet; we are still only getting to know each other' responds the Witch almost dismissively.

The Witch feels the hands of the Moon Goddess take hers and they begin to turn. Slowly at first but then quickening until the pair become a swath of colour dancing from each quadrant of the circle as though paying heed to each of the elements of fire, wind, water and air. As quickly as it all began, so it is ended. The young Witch is standing alone again, and the circle is grounded to allow the circled members to break hands releasing the gathered energy back to the sky.

Sometimes, a night out with friends is all you need and your stress will disappear.

◆ ◆ ◆

Anger Blind

'I've come to see you today Witch to demand a spell to be cast to harm those that have wronged me' speaks the Viking man across the kitchen table. The Witch looks at the man intently. Visually, he looks like he could eat a horse for breakfast if he could find his mouth through his facial hair bush. However, his voice, although rough sounding, sounds of sadness and despair.

The Viking man continues 'I work hard, speaking my gratitude, making offerings daily to the gods, yet I find myself having to prove my value to others daily. These hardships are visited on me by the Great Shaper with no remorse'. The Witch looked across at the Viking man confused. 'So, you would ask me to curse the Great Shaper. How is the Great Shaper to blame for your life lessons or proving yourself?' she asks. 'Shouldn't this be the time to connect with the Grandfather Sun and Mother Earth even more, so you might feel their warmth and support through your struggle?'

The Witch feels the chest muscles of the Viking man tighten as he grips tightly the kitchen table. 'Because the Great One shapes everything, including my hardships. How can I leave offerings or share gratitude when everything I hold dear feels threatened?' he asks.

'But the Great Shaper only helps to bring us teachings we need' said the Witch. 'What is it that you need to learn from these hardships? Perhaps, if you could see that, and still have gratitude for your lessons, your difficulties would dissolve...'.

Muscles twitched in the man's face. 'I have been too angry for that' he snapped slapping the palm of his hand to the table.

The Witch thought for a moment. 'Anger prevents us from our real emotions. Anger sits on top of the real issue and blinds us from true meaning. It also shields our eyes and binds our hearts with hate....' The man listened intently, his eyes darting back and forward in their sockets like a pin ball machine in his head.

'What is beneath your anger?' asks the Witch calmly.

The man thought for a moment his anger slowly ebbing. 'I'm afraid I will not meet the expectations of others' he answers eventually.

The Witch reaches forward across the table and touches the arm of the man. 'Fear can be crippling too, like being stuck in a giant spider web. The more we allow it to paralyse us, the thicker the threads binding us become 'whispers the Witch gently.

The man listened intently occasionally averting his eyes towards the ceiling. 'That's exactly how I feel,' said the man. 'My anger blocks my gratitude and my fear paralyses me to do anything about it'. As he eventually lowers his gaze towards the Witch sitting opposite him to ask, 'What should I do then?'

The moment you feel you must prove yourself to someone else is the moment to walk away.

The Viking Dance Ceremony

'I don't dance very well' she says removing her cloak and stepping forward to take the hand of Pan standing tall before her. Ignoring the comment, he leads her forward into the neon light, the music is playing so loud that own thoughts become hard to hear. The couple are surrounded by others gyrating to a beat that looks like some can only hear in their own minds. The Witch begins to step from one foot to the other, awkwardly, swinging her arms trying to find the rhythm of the music. Just as she finds a rhythm, the music stops, and she finds herself corralled to the centre of the dance floor with all other females of dance age.

As a Witch, she is familiar with Circle Casting with frogsnotpigeons, but this is different and she's not sure where this goes next. She decides to follow the lead of those around her. The outer circle forms by the men. Some appear to be rubbing their hands in expectation, others are just foaming like a racehorse waiting to start a race.

The Witch is part of the surrounded smaller circle that is all women. Doubt aside, the Witch feels the women on either side of her, take her hands in theirs, and the two circles begin to rotate in opposite directions, facing towards each other, to a slow rhythmic beat. This must be some ancient ceremony thinks the Witch silently.

A cursing spell momentarily passes through the mind of the Witch as she sees Pan skip by her in the outer ring clearly enjoying himself. The thought is interrupted only by the stopping of the music. Standing directly opposite the Witch is a large brute. He could easily be a large bale of hay on two legs wearing what looks like a dead sheep thrown across his shoulders. His eyes widen as he looks the Witch's small frame up and down, licking his chops as though eyeing up a fried chicken wing. He steps closer so that his choice of eau de toilette 'parfum du mouton' is evident.

She feels his strength surround her and gasps, partly at the strength of the grip and also at the unexpected loss of her freedom. Her feet dangling in mid-air, her long fingernails dig deep into the man's forearms hoping to put breathing space between them. 'Woah, big boy, can you put me down until we have at least introduced each other?' cries the Witch. The haystack slowly complies and places the Witch back on the floor with the finesse of a dumper truck stuck in first gear.

'Thanks so much, but I think there has been a mistake, Pan will be wondering where I am' shouts the Witch over the music as she dusts the straw and sheep wool from her black clothing. 'Ain't no magic here my dear' gruffs the haystack as he starts his rejection retreat. The Witch scans the sea of moving bodies on the dance floor to see the tallness of Pan clearly interested in the moves of a female wrestler. Her rage grows inside her and a spell is cast before thinking.

Sometimes, life doesn't go to plan and we have to dust ourselves off and move on.

Useless Metaphors

The Witch's days are busy doing spells and the nights watching the shadows for Pan to make an appearance. Each night that he does not appear makes the Witch grow more resentful of the waiting. She knows he had felt drawn to her just as she had said to him. A full moon had come and gone, and she had not heard from him. She checked her WhatsApp again and still no messages. I wonder why some people are lazy with their phones? she wondered.

Looking up from the table, she notices her reflection in the mirror looking back at her. Her mind wanders in her growing frustration as she stares back at her own image in the mirror.

See sees clouds form behind her in the reflection and feels the winter storm close in around her. Shrugging her shoulders to shake of the sudden feeling of cold, she leans closer to the image in the mirror wishing secretly to change what she can see. 'Why are relationships so unreliable?' she whispers to the reflection. After a moment, the Witch hears a voice in the background calling her name in the distance. The reflection darkens and she wonders what this vision is trying to tell her. In the mirror, Pigeons flock around the Witch and she sees the birds circle, fighting against the wind as they look to find a safe place to land before the storm arrives. Frogs are jumping in the foreground as though demented from the constant rain of recent days. The Witch pulls back from the mirror as the Frogs and Pigeons start to fill the reflection more and more so that the Witch's own reflection is becoming faded. In a moment, there is sudden stillness as the creatures quiet. In her reflection, she sees the presence of another take a seat beside her at the table. 'Many do not realize that the moon shines in the day, just as the sun also shines in the night. Both exist doing what they were put here to do; reflect one another. Perhaps that is what relationships are about?' speaks the vison beside her.

The Witch thinks for a milli-second before responding. 'If the Sun had a phone, I'm sure he'd text the Moon to say he'll be around tomorrow as usual!' scowls the Witch folding her arms in front of the mirror.

The Witch purses her lips tightly and looks away as a small tear fills her eye. As she looks back towards the mirror, the visitor smiles and speaks in a soft voice. 'Your thoughts tell you that you are a victim. In turn, the victim speaks of their pain to everyone that will listen even their own reflection. Those that listen will know you suffer, and you will eventually become the martyr to your thoughts. This is the quiet sufferer that pushes the pain and sadness down into the body so that it becomes inner sadness. But there is another way if you choose. Speak open to those you trust and share your unhappiness. Listen well to that which I say Witch, for it is very important'.

A sudden vibration is felt, and the dream is gone. The Witch grabs the mobile phone off the table and reads the message. 'On the Way....'.

If you have someone waiting, pick up the phone and text your on the way.

◆ ◆ ◆

Café Au Lait

'What are you staring at?' snaps the Viking woman from the next table nodding her head in the direction of the Witch. The Witch quickly averts her stare from the two women. The first Viking woman gets to her feet and approaches the Witch's table in a menacing stride. 'Are you deaf Witch?' she roars from her standing position, her hands on the table as though holding the table to the floor. The Witch tries to ignore the Viking but is conscious of the proximity of the woman who could easily reach her from across the table. The Witch looks up at the flaring nostrils of the Viking woman that reminds her of a horse on its last fence at the Grand National. 'I didn't intend offence' she mutters hoping to appease this horse woman back to her stable. 'I just came in for a coffee' she finishes.

'Who do you think your talking to?' roars the Viking woman so that the back of her throat is visible. The spray partially covers the Witch that she has to wipe her face. 'Listen, could you back up a bit?' speaks the Witch. 'I came in for a coffee not a foam and spray' showing the wet palms of her hands to the excited woman standing over her table. The second Viking woman has now also joined at the table and the two women stand over the Witch menacingly as though about to plough a field. 'I just glanced over at you that's all' cries the Witch as she stands to her feet removing her pointed hat. The two women show no signs of letting up. They sense that they have the dominance of size and number superiority. 'You people think you can come and go as you please' shouts the bigger Viking woman as the pair sense their prey's unease. 'Of course, I come and go as I please' responds the Witch. The size advantage of the two Viking women is extreme.

'I don't want any trouble' calls the Witch hoping to get the Vikings to step back. The two Women decide that this is an invitation and lunge towards the Witch. The Witch is surprised by the aggressive move and is unable to avoid the lunging attack. In the following minutes, the scene resembles a cat brawl as the three fall to the floor. Others near, move away for fear of spilling their beverage. Viking men shout as though encouraging the cats to tame the wild shrew, that when cornered, is at its most dangerous. They are to be disappointed as the Witch frees her arms and has already summoned her power. Onlookers quieten as the floor is suddenly swarmed in green frogs, croaking loudly, swarming up through the gaps in the wooden floorboards. The Witch has raised herself from the floor and is standing tall with her arms extended as though about to conduct the final act in a symphony. The two Viking Women shriek from the floor as they are enveloped in the small green creatures. With flaying arms slowly succumbing to the green, a quietness has once again descended on the small café as patrons return to their beverages.

Suddenly, the Witch senses the approach of a another dressed in black. Deliberate and striding towards her with intent. She turns to face the man before her. 'Did you want sugar?' he asks.

Limit your daily caffeine intake and don't stare back at horses.

THE FOUR HORSEMEN

With all the decorations down and the Christmas tree consigned to the garden, the kitchen looks somehow brighter although the greyness of January comes through the window. Sitting at the table, the Witch cups her hands around the hot cup of coffee in front of her and casts her eyes to the reflection staring back from the wall mirror that has re-appeared with the removal of Christmas tinsel. As she sips from her cup, she starts to self-critique the image in the mirror. 'I need to get something done with my hair' she mutters.

Aradia begins to notice the background reflection in the mirror change as though clouding over with crows circling in grey cloud. In her minds eye, she sees four horsemen appear in the reflection background, foreboding of things that have yet to happen. She feels herself drawn into the image and looking around her feels the coldness of January envelop her and she is transported to a wind swept scene in a remote landscape. The Witch feels the coldness against her skin and looks to the first horseman who approaches her. 'Why do you blame others for your misfortune, child'? booms the horseman from his elevated perch. The Witch looks up to the face of criticism.

The second horseman approaches. 'Why do you make excuses and blame others, child'?

Aradia narrowed her eyebrows at the image that created deep furrows across her forehead and raised an anger inside her born out of self-criticism and disappointment. As she stared angrily at her reflection, Aradia leaned back, putting some slack in her shoulders, though she still held her hands on her thighs. 'What is it that you fear, child? What is it that holds you back and from living your dreams'?. The Witch is initially startled and looks around the empty kitchen before turning her gaze back to the mirror. Leaning closer to the mirror, she notices not her own reflection but an image of a grey imp swirling like something from a nightmare that grows arms and fingers and legs and claws and holds her heart with steadfast determination. The image squeezes and flexes its talons just enough so that hopes are still visible, yet souls sink to a place that appears out of reach.

Channel Hopping

Aradia has not yet got over the disappointment of Valentine's day. Sitting at the kitchen table, filing her long nails to near knife edge, she thinks on the disappointment of Pan to signal his affection. A box of black magic, or flowers or simply a card to signal a thought of caring. The Witch feels the tension rise within her as she purses her lips tight at the disappointment of Pan's forgetfulness.

As the doorbell rings, the Witch glances over her shoulder in anticipation – perhaps it's the postman making late deliveries – she thinks to herself wishfully. As she swings open the door, she is immediately disappointed to find it is not a delivery man but a group of cackling witches from the frogsnotpigeons coven. 'Aradia, darling, let us cast a circle tonight for Valentine' cackles the Witching group in unison. Aradia looks down on the assembly of black uniformed crooked noses from her doorstep. Her expression not hiding her disappointment. 'What a pity, but I already have an engagement tonight to clean out the Pigeon Coop' calls a sarcastic Aradia to the gathered ensemble. The Witching group are not convinced by their coven leader's response, and one of the braver nose's shouts 'perhaps you are hoping to meet secretly with Pan tonight?' followed by a chorus of cackles.

The Witch turns quickly. 'Do not mention the name of that man to me' she screams back at the Witching group with distain in her tone that would unnerve a horse. The Witching Group cower at the outburst from their leader. Overhead, clouds have started to gather as though an ominous signal of things to come. Holding firm to the door and the door frame, Aradia bars entry to the house and screams back 'that man, I curse him for mistaking me – Aradia waits for no man'. With that, the door is slammed shut in the faces of the stunned callers and the Witch returns to her lonely anger at the kitchen table.

A voice breaks the silence in the darkness of the room. 'Cold hearted child – tell me how you feel'. The Witch hears but does not respond. The voice repeats, this time louder and with urgency – 'Cold hearted child, tell me how you feel!'

'Perhaps, I will become what I deserve' mutters the Witch softly without looking up from the table. Slowly, slowly, she feels her mind wander to a place of shadows where people live in the confines of their own fears. Shadows call out from the sides 'perhaps', 'what if', 'you can't' and 'fault'.

'Eyes like wild-flowers – only the demons have changed' calls the voice to her mind. The Witch breaths deeply feeling her lungs fill. Exhaling slowly, a sense of peace embraces her. The moment is disturbed as a bell sounds in the distance, like an echo calling to follow. Efforts to ignore are refused as the bell sounds again.

The Witch feels a strong physical presence approach to her side. As her mind slowly focuses, a tall uniform man reaches towards her as bright colours come into focus.

'I believe these are for you' speaks the man placing the wild-flowers on the table.

Sometimes, we place ourselves in a story line that is created by our own imagination coloured by our doubts and fears. If you find yourself in the wrong story, of fear, of constraints, of doubts and worry. Change channel.

The Coming of The Switchman

'I hear the cries of sorrow and loss approaching' responds the Witch back to the assembled before her. The assembled group look on for inspiration and hope from their last hope. They know that the growing sound signals the approach of the Switchman. Out on the horizon, large clouds of darkness like smoke lift into the air. All those gathered know that soon the darkness will be fire.

'Tell us what we must do Aradia – to prepare for the coming night and protect ourselves' calls the village elder. The Witch looks back across the assembly of doubt filled faces that dare call her name. Turning her gaze back to the distant horizon, the Witch turns inwards to hear her own mind. Fate whispers to her thoughts, 'you cannot withstand the coming storm'.

'I am the storm' calls the Witch above the rising wind. 'It is time to cast the circle for those who choose to turn to the night with me. The rest that don't, must wait their fate that I cannot hold for them'. As the Witch raises her staff to the darkening sky, she knows that she will need all her magic tonight.

Soon after, the assembled has dispersed, each to their own. Those remaining are few, but has their own magic to bring to the circle. As the circle is formed, the hooded gathered touches the earth in turn to ground the circle before casting an offering to the fire spirit. Flames reach high into the darkening sky with embers rising into the blackness like a million stars in a rush to find their place in the coming night dance. The circle is cast.

The hooded gathered close the circle with a chain of inter-twined hands – the chant begins to summon the four guardians of the watchtowers. 'East then South, then West then North' rings out across the darkening expanse as those gathered cry out to the blackness surrounding them. The Witch dances wildly with blackened feet around the fire, staff in hand her arms raised sky-wards to welcome spirits from the sky. As the chanting ebbs, the Witch drops her arms to her side and places the staff to the ground. The assembled circle of hooded members begins to lift from the damp earth – holding tight to outstretched arms the bodily circle begins to turn slowly in a clockwise motion. Each of the assembled looks to hang from the sky by some invisible thread, bare feet pointing down to the earth, members joined only by outstretched arms holding hands. Each cry out in unison, 'we travel to the darkness and endure, we walk with the fearless-ness of the Wolf, the bravery of the Lion and fierceness of the Dragon'.

The Witch at the centre opens her mouth to release the loud high-pitched scream of Aradia that carries far and signals the arrival of the Storm. Soon, she thinks, we will meet the Switchman in person.

When we have travelled to the darkness and endured, we become stronger. Walk with the fearlessness of the Wolf, the bravery of the Lion and the fierceness of the Dragon. Be the Storm...

In the Stars

Recent nights are disturbed as the Banshee makes her presence known to all that hear. Her sound is that of death song and makes for unease among the frogsnotpigeons gathered. 'Why must we hear this wailing cry?' complains loudest of the hooded. 'Surely, this forsaken soul knows we are here for those who cannot?'

The Witch opens her eyes, sleep wanting, and looks to the direction of the gathered. 'The Banshee is doing what she must as do we', she whispers. 'Be thankful you can hear her song for that means you are not yet seated at her table. We are destined to be here and soon will our fate be told'. The darkness has fallen across the assembly and they feel the Switchman again draw near. Outside, the sky burns from the horizon to high in the sky and the air is heavy with those that have already fallen. Each of the frogsnotpigeons gathered hope that the Banshee does not call to them in the coming hours.

The Switchman commands a gathering of sorrowful souls who have surrendered choice following his bidding. They beat a sound on their shields to invite those that oppose to meet them. Aradia knows that tonight she must meet The Switchman face to face. For a moment, Aradia looks around her circle and sees the ashen faces of the gathered few who stand with her as the guardians of choice and freewill against the ensemble of those intent on taking what is not theirs to own. The ensuing chant grows louder than their voices alone and soon fills the smoking sky above. 'Darksome Night and Shining Moon, East then South, then West then North, here we stand to call thee forth' rings so loud that all can hear. A scream follows each round of chant to send the call even higher to the sky. Above the Witch's circle, the storm gathers and a thousand stars peer down on them through the blackness.

In a moment, the Witch feels the veil of darkness close across her face as an invisible force lifts her to the sky. She feels a rush of wind against her face. A sudden silence falls in this quiet place. Aradia slowly opens her eyes that focus quickly on a presence before her. Slowly, she steps forward from the surrounding darkness into the light and the Witch looks upon the tallness of the Switchman. Never surprised, he turns slowly to face the Witch. Slowly, he lifts his eyes to meet hers – a steel grey piercing look.

'All have the stars. For some who are travellers the stars are guides. For others, they are just lights in the night sky. For me, I read the stars that tell me my destiny is to be here in this place' speaks the Switchman.

'I am the Witch of the Tuatha De, tribe of the gods. I write the story in the stars as no one else' whispers the Witch.

What is written in the stars is not the story you were born for. Each of us decides what is written in the stars for us. This is called your destiny. Choose it carefully.

◆ ◆ ◆

Who Needs Friends ?

Numbed by the cold and the passing of time, the Witch knows that all is not as it should. Soon, her senses start to sharpen, and she feels the pain of a battle she has not won. Her mind races to recall how she came to be here on this floor facing skywards. She realizes that she is unable to lift herself from this alter of despair. She is alone.

A sound signals the approach of another climbing the stairs purposely to eventually stand over the Witch. The Switchman, steps over the fallen prey as though to validate his conquest and walks purposely around her. Each of his steps deliberate, like a heavy shod horse, he sounds on the floorboards that echo through the Witch's stiffened body signalling fear and pain.

The Witch's mind is filled with the unknown and hopeless scenarios playout in the Witch's mind as she recalls the previous days lost effort. She feels her lungs small and her breath shallow from her piercing wound. Her strength stretches to opening her eyes to look up at the shadowy figure above her. His eyes glint from the darkness of his hooded face and the Witch recognizes the figure as the ghost she has seen in every mirror, the Switchman. 'Speak your intention' forces the Witch from her cracked lips. The demand goes unanswered – instead a mocking smile returns from the assuming victor.

The Witch cries out, louder, more urgently, forceful. 'Speak' she cries to be heard above the wind. The Switchman drops a knee to the floor and places his cold face near to the Witch that she can feel the staleness of his breath against her cheek. He whispers to her. 'There is a sadness in this world, but it is weariness that lies at the heart of mine. When I take yours, I will finish the passion that makes you burn bright.'

Across the darkness, in the distance, a scream of a familiar sounds loudly. 'The Banshee is calling to you Witch, soon you will meet her face to face', whispers the Switchman before standing to his feet looking out to the distance towards the direction of the wailing woman, like all men, hypnotised by her cry. The Witch turns her head away as much as she can fearing what she does not know. In the smallest corner of her eye, she sees the blue grey of a familiar bird. Its feathers bluster in the wind as though fighting to hold position. For a moment, the Witch thinks perhaps her last and closes her eyes reserved to her fate as the Banshee cries out the final call.

In the seconds that pass, a darkness envelope's the Witch as she curses the wail of the Banshee and her impatience. Around her she feels hands of many touching on her skin and a feeling that she knows. The Witch's eyes flash to the presence of the hooded that swarm around her in a cloud of feathers and smoke. Standing to her feet she holds out her outstretched open hand to feel the Witch's blade handle fill her palm. 'The frogsnotpigeons have found me' she whispers.

Never take for granted your friends and family. The time will come soon when you will need them most.

Living History.

'You will never set foot here again' whispers the Witch Aradia still holding tight grip of the blade hilt buried deep into the Switchman. The Switchman makes no discernible response except to force a last breath like he has done to many others. As he makes his passing, the darkness begins to lift. Aradia looks away from the ailing figure to see the grey faces of her own frogsnotpigeons. The circled group of hooded gazes down on the scene of both victory and relief. The only sound is the murmurings from those of the circle who continue to recite in unison the prayer of destiny.

Overhead, dark clouds start to lift and there is the appearance of a new dawn. The Witch stands slowly to her feet covered in the life blood of the Switchman that now covers the floor of where they stand. Aradia turns to each of the gathered as though to silently acknowledge them before taking her place centre circle. Raising her arms, with palms skywards as though holding up an invisible weight, she joins in the chanting voices that grow to become louder and louder until suddenly ending to silence.

The silence is broken only by the chorus of claps and cheers from the survivors and they realise their redemption. 'We are done here' calls the Witch to her followers as she grounds the circle to let the followers break their hand chains and release the circle. Once released, the Witch notices the silhouette of a horseman dismount and walk slowly towards her. The group opens freely to let him enter and the Witch recognizes one of the many faces of Pan standing before her. The Witch draws a deep breath that fills her lungs and slowly releases as though to set the breath free finally. Turning to the motionless figure of the Switchman laying still at her feet – she watches as Pan lifts the body from the floor and places across his sky horse unceremoniously. 'Today, Aradia, you have out-shone even the stars' speaks Pan slowly turning to face the Witch. Lifting her eyes to meet his, she shakes her head from one side to the other that lifts her wild hair so to eventually fall to one shoulder. 'I once had a dream that life was as a comet travelling across the night sky. It moved at such a speed, as though in a rush to meet its final destiny' speaks Aradia in a soft tone. 'I woke so frightened with tears in my eyes for all those who wait its arrival' she whispered softly.

Pan looks down on the smallness of the Witch who defeated the demon Switchman that brought sadness to many. He couldn't help but think of all the villagers that unknowingly owed their safety to a few. In years to come, others will study this time we live in.

They will learn how rainbows were a sign of hope. They will hear how people came together to cheer and clap the amazing people who saved lives and kept our country safe. They will hear stories of a time where the world slowed down, polluted skies cleared, and fish reclaimed rivers and streams. A time when we treasured being able to get out for a walk once a day. We are living through history now. How will you remember it?

We are frogsnotpigeons…. Stay Safe.

DEREK FINN

ABOUT THE AUTHOR

Derek Finn

Derek is a holds a Post Grad in Computer Science from WIT and a Post Grad in Applied Psychology from University College Cork.

BOOKS BY THIS AUTHOR

Wildest Moments

Short Stories of morality told with humor and sacrasm. Set in the time of the Pandemic, these stories take you through social isolation and the spirit of a community joined through a common goal.

Alice's Mind

This is an adult book that blends psychology and fiction. The story is about Alice B who likes to people watch. Using dreams, Alice B starts to play mind games with others until she eventually looses her own mind.

Made in the USA
Las Vegas, NV
08 September 2021